HUMOR
for
MATURE MINDS

Volume 1

Not your typical joke book

WILLIAM (BILL) DAUGHERTY LLC

iUniverse, Inc.
Bloomington

Humor for Mature Minds, Volume 1
Not your typical joke book

iUniverse books may be ordered through booksellers or by contacting:

iUniverse
1663 Liberty Drive
Bloomington, IN 47403
www.iuniverse.com
1-800-Authors (1-800-288-4677)

ISBN: 978-1-4759-8321-0 (sc)
ISBN: 978-1-4759-8322-7 (ebk)

Library of Congress Control Number: 2013905625

Printed in the United States of America

iUniverse rev. date: 04/04/2013

Contents

Preface

There are too few good story tellers. But most everyone can tell a good story with practice. I would recommend you consider this book as a primer.

Pick two or three jokes or stories at a time. Memorize them and practice their presentation, being conscious of the timing and voice inflections. Then, when you're ready, tell the joke; you'll have the benefit of hearing the story and the appreciative response of the audience.

Laughter is good for both body and soul. Spread it around

Bill Daugherty

1. The Skiers

On December 22nd, friends Tom and John decide to go skiing over the Christmas holidays. As they drive to the slopes, a light snow shower becomes heavier.

"Tom," John says, "there's a large ranch house a head. Why don't we stop and ask them if they could put us up until this snow stops? I'm afraid if we go much further, we could be stranded."

"Sounds good to me."

They walk up the path and ring the doorbell.

A beautiful woman answers, and asks what they want.

'Ma'am," Tom replies, "we were on our way to the ski slopes when this snow began. We're worried about continuing, and wondered if you could put us up for the night?"

"Of course, gentlemen. However, I'm a widow. People might talk if you stayed in the house. I do have a couple of beds in the tack-room in the stable behind the house. It's heated, and bedclothes are in the closet. Drive around back, and put your car in the carport. The entrance is in the breezeway between the buildings. The tack room is on the right."

"Thank you, Ms . . . ?" Tom questions.

"Deborah Billings."

"Ms. Billings," he continues, "if it clears up, we'll leave early, so we'll thank you now for your hospitality."

*   *   *

About nine months later, John receives a thick packet of papers from the woman's attorney. After perusing the material, he picks up his cell phone and calls Tom.

"Hi, John, what's up?"

"Tom, do you remember on our Christmas trip when we stopped at the ranch owned by that beautiful woman?"

"Of course, why do you ask?"

"Tom, did you sneak out, go to the house and make love to that woman?"

Yes, John, I did."

"Did you give her my name instead of yours?"

"Yes. Are you in trouble?"

"No! She died and left the ranch and fifty million dollars to me . . . . Tom? . . . Are you there, Tom."

2. The Little Nun

While sitting in the physician's waiting room a woman notices a young nun with a severe case of hiccups.

Shortly after being called into the examining room, the nun screams, "NO!" then runs, crying hysterically, out of the office.

The nurse beckons to the other woman, and says, "You're next Mrs. Jones,"

"Doctor, if I may ask, what did you tell to the poor girl that made her so upset?"

"I told her she was pregnant."

"Really?"

"No, but it cured her hiccups."

3. Good Driver of the Month

A cop has been tailing a car for several miles after it crossed the border from Mexico into the U.S. at San Ysidro. Finally, he pulls ahead of the vehicle, and directs the driver to pull over.

The driver rolls down the window, and asks, "What did I do wrong, officer?"

"Nothing, sir. I've observed you for some time, and you have followed every traffic law and speed limit. You're our Safe Driver of the Month. You'll receive a good driver certificate and a $200 cash award. What will you do with the money?"

The driver thinks for a moment, and says, "I think I'd better use it for driving lessons, so I can get a license."

Just then, the woman in the front seat leans over and remarks, "Don't pay no attention to him officer; he always gets smart-alecky when he's drunk"

The man in the back seat wakes up, and, upon seeing the cop, says, "I told you we wouldn't get far in a stolen car!"

Just then, a voice from the trunk inquires, "Are we across the border yet, senor?"

4. To Cure or Not to Cure

An Irishman in a wheelchair rolls into a restaurant and up to a table. As he orders a doughnut and coffee, he notices a man with long hair, clothed in a sheet-like garment. "Faith," he exclaims, "is that me Lord Jesus?"

The waitress nods in agreement.

"Give the man some bacon and eggs, and put it on me bill."

An Englishman, with a humpback, enters, sits down in a booth, and orders a full English breakfast. He, too, asks if the bearded man is Jesus.

The waitress confirms his observation.

"Give the man pie á la mode, and add it to my check, please."

A redneck comes in, hopping on crutches. He, too, inquires if the man in the sheet is Jesus.

The waitress agrees with his assumption, he says, "Give the man a Coke, and add it to my bill."

When Jesus finishes hi meal, he walks to the Irishman, lays his hand on the man's shoulder, and says, "Arise, your paralysis is cured."

Turning to the Englishman, he touches his hump, and it disappears.

As Jesus strides over to the redneck, the man screams, "Don't touch me—I'm drawin' disability."

5. Dear Proctor and Gamble

Dear Proctor and Gamble,

I want to compliment you on your most excellent product, Tide. I am in my fifties, and going through menopause. It seems important for me to tell you that. The other night, I inadvertently spilled wine on my new blouse. My obnoxious, over-bearing husband, vehemently chastised me for my clumsiness. To make a long story short, I ended up with blood and wine stains on my blouse. I immediately reached for the Tide, and bleach alternative, to wash my blouse.

The DNA tests came out negative, and I am no longer a suspect.

I must go now, and write a letter to the Hefty Bag people.

Sincerely,
Annie Slaughter

6. Murphy Ties One On Again

Murphy has been sitting on a barstool, imbibing, in Clancy's bar. Clancy announces, "Closin' time. Everybody out."

Murphy slid off the stool and collapsed on the floor. *Ooooh*, he says to himself, *I must have had more to drink than I thought.* Slowly, he crawls to the door and hoists himself up the jamb. *I think I'll just lean against here a bit. Maybe the fresh air will clear me head.*

Murphy finally steps away from the door and falls on his face. *Begorra, I think I'd better crawl home, 'tis only four doors to me house.*

When he arrives home, he pulls himself up the stairs. Somehow, he unlocks the door, and is able to undress and climb into bed.

The next morning, Mrs. Murphy confronts him. "Ye really tied one on again last night, didn't ye?"

"Woman, how can ye say a thing like that?"

"Clancy called. Ye left your wheelchair at his bar again."

7. Billy's Grandma

Grandma is babysitting her grandson, Billy. Billy comes in from play with his friends, and asks, "Grandma, what do they call it when two people sleep in the same room, and one sleeps on top of the other?"

Grandma thinks for a moment, and remembers reading that you are supposed to answer such questions simply and truthfully, so she replies, "Billy, it's called sexual intercourse." That explanation seems to satisfy him and his friends, and they dash out to play again.

Soon, he returns and says, "You're wrong, grandma. It's called bunk-beds, and Timmy's mom wants to talk to you."

8. Dumb Blonde Joke # 17

A blonde is driving her Audi convertible at 85 mph where the speed limit is 60. A blonde motorcycle cop flashes her red lights, and waves the Audi to pull over to the side of the road.

"You were doing 85 in a 65 mile per hour zone. May I see your license, please?"

"Yes, officer, it's in my purse." The driver fumbles around in the contents, then asks, "What does it look like?"

"It's rectangular and has your picture on it," replies the blonde cop.

Again the driver rummages around in her purse, she takes out a mirror, looks into it, hands it to the cop, and says, "Here you are, officer."

The cop looks at it and remarks, "I didn't know you're a cop." She hands it back to the driver and says, "Sorry I stopped you. Drive on."

9. Really Big Problems

A man sits at the bar, moaning over and over, "What am I going to do?"

The Bartender comes up to him and declares, "Normally, I don't get involved with my patron's problems, but you sound like you really need someone to talk to. "What's your problem, buddy?"

The man motions toward a woman at one end of the bat, and whispers, "That's my wife."

"My God, fella, she's absolutely beautiful. What's your problem?"

Gesturing to the other end of the bar, the man quietly replies, "That's my mistress."

"Aw, come on; you have a beautiful wife, and an equally beautiful mistress. How can you have a problem?"

Pointing out the door, the man says, "That's my car parked at the entrance.

The bartender, becoming a bit irritated, says, "Gee fella, I'd like to sympathize with you, but what have you got to complain about? You have a beautiful wife, a gorgeous mistress, and a Rolls-Royce Silver Cloud. What the hell do you have to complain about?"

The man replies, "They're all three months overdue."

10. Disgruntled Passenger

The stewardess races up the aisle toward the commotion at the front of the plane. A man's irritated voice spits out, "I hate this damn airline! I always get the same seat! It doesn't recline! There's no shade on my window, and I can't see the movie!"

The stewardess leans over and quietly states, "Shut up and just fly the plane, Captain."

11. The World Is Misbehaving

A person tells the following joke.

The archangel reports to God that 80% of earthlings are misbehaving.

God doubts so many could be transgressing, and decides to send another angel to earth to verify the number.

A week later the angel reappears, "God," he reports, "the archangel is right—80% of the people of earth are misbehaving."

God declares, "I must send a message to the 20% congratulating them for not succumbing to the temptations of the other 80%."

The joke teller then asks his audience, "Do you know what the message said?"

He follows with, "I didn't get the message either."

12. The Missing Gravy Ladle

John calls his mother. "Mom, I'm calling to tell you I found a roommate to share the expenses for my apartment. We'd like you to come to dinner, Sunday, so you can meet her."

"Her? Your roommate is a her?"

"Don't worry, Mom. It's a business proposition. She has her bedroom, and I have mine. We split the costs and chores right-down-the-middle. Would five o'clock be all right?"

"Of course, son. I want to meet this woman."

His mother arrives and is introduced to Julie, who proves to be a very pretty, petite woman.

The two of them show his mother their separate bedrooms. "See, Mother, we have our own bedrooms."

After dinner, his parent returns home.

Two days later, Julie says, "I hate to say this John, but since your mother was here, I haven't been able to find the silver gravy ladle."

"I'm sure my mother would never steal a gravy ladle, but I'll call her tomorrow."

"Mom," he says when he calls, "I'm not saying you did take the silver gravy ladle, I'm not saying you didn't take it. But ever since you were here, we can't find it."

"Son," she replies, "I'm not saying you're sleeping with Julie; I'm not saying you aren't sleeping with Julie. But if she were sleeping in her own bed, she would have found that damn gravy ladle."

13. Sisters of Charity House of Prostitution

A man, driving from Tucson to Phoenix, decides to stop for gas and lunch at an off-road station. Following lunch, as he drives along the frontage road back to the highway, he spies a large sign at the turn-off, reading; "Sisters of Charity House of Prostitution, five miles," with an arrow pointing to the right, away from the highway.

Well, I never heard of that before, I think I'll see what it's all about. He drives along the road and is confronted by another sign; this one reads; "Sisters of Charity House of Prostitution, one mile."

Soon, another sign says: "Sisters of Charity House of Prostitution, turn right." He enters a parking lot where another sign reads: "Park Here, Enter at Front." An arrow points toward a path to the entrance. As he starts toward the entrance, behind the sign he notices a path leading to a small door in the side of the convent.

Proceeding to the front, he opens a large door, and encounters a nun sitting behind a desk.

"What can I do for you, sir?" she questions.

"I saw your sign and thought I'd see what it's all about."

"Like it says, it's about prostitution. The cost is $100."

"OK," he replies, "I'll try it."

The elderly nun rings a bell, and a lovely young nun answers, "You rang, Sister Grace?"

"Yes. This man wishes to partake in the pleasures of our house. Will you please entertain him?"

"Of course, sister. Please follow me, sir." She leads him down a long corridor, unlocks a door, and tells him to enter. Then she unlocks another door and asks him to step through. He complies, and hears the click of the lock behind him. He walks out, and finds himself outside in the parking lot. Written on the back of the sign he'd seen when he parked his car is: "You've just been screwed by the Sisters of Charity. Have a good day!"

14. Cat Heaven

A cat dies, and enters heaven. St Peter asks if the cat has any special requests.

"Yes, sir. All my life I've had to sleep on the cold, hard floor of the barn. I'd really like a soft, warm place to sleep."

"So be it," says St. Peter, and he gives the cat a big, soft pillow near a warm fireplace.

Later, four mice enter heaven. St Peter asks if they have any special requests.

"Yes," said the mice. "We've always had to run, run, run. We'd like to find a way to get around without running."

St. Peter replies, "I think I have the answer," and he gives each of them roller-skates. The mice are pleased and skate off.

After a few days, St Peter is making his rounds and comes across the cat, lying on its pillow. "How's everything, cat?"

"Just wonderful, sir. For the first time, I'm warm and very comfortable. By the way, those meals on wheels are a nice touch."

15. Wife for the Night

Mr. Jones, and his secretary, Miss Smith, were on a business trip. As a result of a weather delay, they arrive at their destination very late in the evening. The desk clerk informed them there was only one room left and it had two double beds. He wondered if they would consider sharing the room.

They talked it over, and decided that because of the late hour, they had no choice but to share the room.

Jones said, "Miss Smith, you go up now, and I'll come up in a half hour. Will that give you sufficient time to get into bed?"

"Yes, sir."

Jones dawdles in the bar, and then, thirty minutes later, he comes up and goes to bed.

Shortly, Miss Smith says, "Mr. Jones, I'm cold."

Jones gets up and brings a blanket from the closet. He spreads it over the woman and returns to bed.

A few minutes later, Miss Smith utters a plaintive cry, "Mr. Jones, I'm still cold."

Jones thinks for a minute, and replies, Miss Smith, would you like to pretend you're Mrs. Jones for tonight?"

'Oh, yes, sir. I'd like that."

"Good! Get up and close the damn window."

16. The Skin Graft

A man and his wife were in a terrible accident. The wife sustained a broken arm, but the man's face was severely burned.

It was determined, after consulting with the plastic surgeon, the man's body could not be the source of a suitable facial skin graft; however, after considerable discussion, it was ascertained that the wife's buttocks could provide a graft of sufficient size to cover the burn scars. The wife readily volunteered, but said she and her husband insisted upon complete secrecy as to the graft donor.

After recovering from the operation, people raved about how wonderful he looked. Some thought he was more handsome now than he had before the accident.

"Darling," he said, "how can I ever repay you for the skin graft you provided for me?"

"Lover," she replied, "I get rewarded every time I see your mother kiss you on your cheek."

17. Bubba's Venison Barbeque

Before WWII, Bubba lived next to the Catholic Church, and every Friday he'd cook up a savory barbecue of venison.

The priest talked to Bubba and explained the problems he was creating among parishioners by barbecuing venison every Friday. "Bubba, we are prohibited from eating meat on Friday, and the delicious smell of your barbecue is sorely tempting my people to come over and join you. Couldn't you please do your cooking on another day, or change the menu to fish?"

"I'm sorry, Father, this has been a tradition in my family for over a hundred years."

"Maybe if you converted to Catholicism, you could see your way to avoid cooking meat on Fridays."

"Well, Father, if you think it would help, I'd be pleased to become a Catholic."

After several lessons, the priest sprinkled holy water over Bubba and said, "You were born a Baptist, you were raised a Baptist, but now you are Catholic."

However, the next Friday, Bubba was again cooking his venison.

The priest stormed over to Bubba's backyard, and observed him sprinkling water over the meat, intoning, "You was born a deer, you was raised a deer, but now you is catfish."

18. An Easy Call

A drunk was standing in a grocery line behind a woman who had placed her order on the conveyor belt, "Ma'am," he said, "You're not married, are you?"

She looked down at the food she had purchased: milk, sugar, eggs, a loaf of bread, and a head of lettuce. She could see nothing to indicate she wasn't married. "Yes, I'm single. How did you know?"

"Cause you're ugly."

19. Government Bureaucracy

A woman purchased several hundred acres of virgin redwood forest to keep it from being destroyed by a lumber company. She drove into the forest to survey her new holdings, and decided to climb up the tallest tree to get a view of her property. After much effort, she grasped a limb to pull herself up, disturbing a spotted owl that flew directly toward her face. She was so startled she released her hold and slid all the way down the tree.

The slide resulted in splinters of redwood piercing her arms, legs and torso. Painfully, she drove her car down to town, and stopped at a local doctor's office. Hobbling into the waiting room, she told the receptionist of her problem and intense pain. The girl took her into an examination room, and told her the doctor would see her immediately.

Not a minute went by before the doctor entered and gave her an examination. "Ma'am, I must take care of something very important first, I'll return as quickly as possible."

The woman fumed as the minutes ticked by. Finally, after two hours, the doctor reappeared. "Where the hell have you been? I'm in agony, and you make me wait for two hours?"

"I thought I did rather well. I had to get permits."

"What permits?"

"Before I could operate, I had to get them from the Environmental Protection Agency, the Forestry Department, and the Department of Parks and Recreation."

"Why"

"In order to remove old growth timber from a recreational area."

20. The Portrait

An elderly woman was in a hospice knowing full-well she was dying. Her husband asked, "My dearest, you've been a wonderful wife these past fifty years. Is there anything you want before you die?"

"Yes," she replied, "I'd like to have my portrait painted,"

"Of course, dear. I'll have an artist here this afternoon."

The artist arrived, and asked what pose she wanted for the portrait.

"I want to be in a light-blue satin gown, with a black-velvet background. I'd like a diamond tiara in my hair, diamond earrings, a diamond necklace, and a diamond lavaliere pinned to the left shoulder."

"Dearest, you don't have any diamonds. Why would you want the man to paint them in your portrait?"

"I want your next wife to go crazy looking for the jewels."

21. The Smart Blonde

A blonde woman enters a bank on Friday, just before closing time, and asks to see the manager.

"I know this is a very strange request, but I have to take a trip to Europe tomorrow, and I need a loan of $5,000 today."

The manager looked at her and said, "I'm sorry madam, you're not a customer, and I can't take a chance of loaning you $5,000."

"I'll tell you what, sir, I'll leave my $150,000 Mercedes as collateral. I'll be back next week."

When she returns, the bank manager hands her a bill for $15.40 to cover the interest on the loan. "Tell me ma'am, why would you leave such a valuable car as collateral for a week's loan of $5,000?"

"Where else could I safely leave my car for a week for $15.40?"

22. Abstinence

Three couples—newlyweds, middle-aged, and seniors—applied for membership in the local church. The minister said, "Membership in our congregation is an important decision, requiring sacrifice, determination, and honesty. Consequently, before we admit you to membership, we require each couple to pass a test to validate their strength of character. We require you to forego sex for a month. I'll see you all in thirty days. Good luck."

After the requisite time had passed, the three couples appeared before the minister. "Well, how did you fare?"

The seniors replied, "We've been married forty years, and had no problem abstaining from sex for the thirty days."

"Fine,' said the minister, "welcome to our congregation."

The middle-aged couple reported, "We had a tough time after three weeks, but we were able to stick-it-out for the month."

"Welcome to our church."

Turning to the newlyweds he inquired, "Were you able to meet the requirements?"

"I'm afraid not." the man replied. "We did OK for the first two weeks, and then one night at dinner, Mary dropped her fork on the floor. As we both bent down to retrieve it, I looked at her, and she looked at me, and we had sex right there."

"I'm sorry,' the minister sternly replied, "you can't become members of our church."

"That's OK, sir. Denny's doesn't want us either."

Alternate ending. "After they told us to stop, I told them your sign says this is a family restaurant and we were starting a family."

23. Murphy Argues with His Wife

Patrick Murphy entered the bar and called out, "Sean, fix me a stiff one. I just had another fight with me wife."

"How'd it turn out?"

"I had her on her hands and knees."

"What did she say/"

'Come out from under the bed, ye coward!"

24. Mrs. Shirley Goodness

Two first graders were walking to school, when one asked, "Have you noticed the woman and little girl who follow us to school every day?"

"Yes," replied the other boy, "that's Mrs. Shirley Goodness and her daughter Marcie. They're our next-door neighbors."

"Why are they following us?"

"My mom worries about me. So they see that we get to school safely."

"Gee, how long will this go on?"

"Forever, I guess. I'll just have to get used to it. Every night my mom reads the 23rd Psalm, You know, 'Shirley Goodness and Marcie will follow you all the days of thy life.'"

25. Jesus is Watching

A burglar entered the seemingly unoccupied house. As he reached for a silver candelabra, a weird voice intoned, "Jesus is watching you."

Startled, the burglar looked around. Seeing no one, he picked up the candelabra again. The voice spoke once more, "Jesus is watching you."

This time the man slowly searched the room with his flashlight and illuminated a parrot on a stand. "Who are you?" he inquired.

"Moses," replies the bird.

"What kind of a jackass would name a parrot Moses?"

"The same one who names his pit bull Jesus. Sic him Jesus."

26. Elderly Sisters

Three sisters of 90, 88, and 86 years old, respectively, lived together in the house of their childhood. The 90 year-old called out, "Was I getting into the bath or out of the bath?"

The 88 year-old said, "I'll be right up to tell you." When she got to the landing, she asked her younger sister, "Was I going up the stairs or down the stairs?"

The younger sister said to herself, "I hope I never get that forgetful, knock-on-wood." Then she called to her sister on the stairs, "I'll tell you after I see who's knocking at the door."

27. Smart-ass Parrot

A woman, walking through a mall, passed a pet store. A parrot called out, "Hey, lady."

She stopped, and replied, "Yes?"

The parrot said, "You're ugly."

Highly agitated, the woman continued on her way. Upon her return, she was again passing the pet store, when the parrot again called out, "Hey, lady."

The woman stopped, and, with a stern expression, replied, "What do you want?"

"You're still ugly," the bird chortled.

The woman snatched the bird by its legs, and took it screaming and flapping to the store owner. She snarled, "This bird insulted me twice by calling me ugly. If it happens again, I'll wring its neck and sue you for harassment. Do you understand?"

"Yes, ma'am. I'll make sure he never says it again. I apologize for his bad behavior."

A few days later the woman again passed the pet store, and the parrot called out, "Hey, lady."

The woman looked at the bird and replied, "Yes?"

The parrot twitched his left shoulder, winked, and said, "You know."

28. Three Nuns on the Train

Three nuns are traveling together on a train. During the journey they decided to tell their secret vices.

The first nun said, "When I'm on leave, I become a prostitute, but I give all the money to the poor."

The second stated, "When I'm on vacation, I go on a binge and drink myself into a stupor."

The third giggled and informed them, "I'm an inveterate gossip, and I can't wait to get off this train."

29. Ole and Lena

Ole, who was not much of a church-goer, attended Easter services, and was greatly attracted to Lena, one of the Sunday school teachers. He became a regular attendee, and eventually got up the nerve to ask her for a date. She accepted an invitation to dinner the following Saturday.

As they sat down to dinner, Ole asked, "Lena, would you like a cigarette?"

"Oh, no," she replied. "What would I tell my Sunday school children?"

After dinner, Ole inquired, "Lena, would you care for an after-dinner drink?"

"Oh, no," she exclaimed. "What would I tell my children?"

On the way back to her home, they were passing a motel, and Ole, who figured he'd already struck out, asked, "Lena, would you consider spending the night in the motel?"

To his great surprise, she gave an enthusiastic, "Yes!"

The following morning, Ole asked, "Lena, what will you tell your children?"

"I'll tell them you don't have to drink or smoke to have a good time."

30. Lug Nuts

A man had a flat tire outside of an insane asylum. As he changed the tire, he noticed one of the patients watching him from behind the bars of a fence surrounding the building.

The man removed the spare tire from the trunk, jacked up the car, and removed the lug nuts. He placed them in the wheel cover and set it aside in the road. After removing the flat tire he placed it in the trunk. As he walked back to put on the spare, a car drove by, and clipped the wheel cover, flipping the lug nuts into the weeds.

The man, unsuccessful at finding the nuts, said aloud to himself, "Now, what can I do? I can't put the spare on."

The patient who had watched the entire proceedings, said, "Why don't you take a lug nut from each of the other wheels? That should enable you to get to a filling station where they can put new nuts on the wheels."

The man looked at the patient and observed, "That's brilliant! What are you doing in the asylum?"

The patient replied, "I'm crazy—not stupid."

31. Socialized Medicine

A man and his wife emigrated to England. During the first trimester of her pregnancy the woman went for a checkup at their local hospital, and had her first experience with socialized medicine. After her examination, the physician pressed a stamp on an indelible ink pad and then pressed the stamp against her stomach, telling her to follow the directions on the stamp, and left.

When her husband arrived home that evening, he asked how the examination went.

"I don't know. The doctor told me to follow the directions on my stomach, but I can't read them; the print is too small."

"Let me get a magnifying glass. I should be able to read the printing with it."

The stamp read, "When you can read this with the naked eye, come in and I'll deliver the baby."

32. The Foursome

A man walked up to the starter at a golf course and inquired, "Do you have an opening for a single?"

The starter motioned toward three men waiting on the first tee. "Why don't you ask them if they'd mind if you joined them?"

The fellow asked the three men if he could play with them.

"Of course. And, if you care to participate, we play for a dollar a hole, with carryovers."

"Sure. Count me in."

"Well, son," one of the men asked, "what's your handicap?"

"I haven't played in a while. I've got a stiff back," he said, hunching his shoulder. "I guess around a five."

Back in the locker room, after the game, the young man was gleefully counting his winnings when he noticed something strange about the three men he'd played with; they were putting their collars on backward. He recognized they were priests, and walked up to them and said, "Gentlemen, I can't take money from priests. Here, take it back."

"No," one of them replied. "Any man with a five handicap who shoots two under par deserves the money. By the way, are your parents in town?"

"Yes, sir."

"Send them around tomorrow, and I'll marry them."

33. American in England

An American climbed aboard a train in London, bound for Birmingham. The only remaining seat was occupied by a small fuzzy dog seated next to a stern-looking dowager. "Ma'am," he inquired, "would you please hold your dog, as I am very tired?"

She replied, "No. This dog is a grand champion, whose pedigree spans 600 years. She has more right to this seat than you do."

As the train pulled out of the station and sped toward its destination, the man made a final request. "Ma'am, please hold your dog so I may sit down."

"I could not be more emphatic. The answer is no."

Without another word, the American reached over and dropped the sash, grabbed the dog, threw it out the window, and sat down.

Another man in the compartment went, "Tich, tich, tich. You Americans are all alike. You threw the wrong bitch out the window."

34. A Short Story for the Teacher

One day, the English teacher who wanted some time to grade papers, instructed the class, "Today, I want you to write a story embodying the following four subjects: deity, royalty, sex, and mystery.

"That should keep them busy," she thought, "while I grade these papers."

No sooner did she look at the first paper, when Johnny raised his hand.

"What do you want, John?"

"I'm finished," he responded.

"Already? Bring your paper to me, and I'll see how well you complied with my directions."

Johnny handed her his paper. It read, "My God, the queen's pregnant—who done it?"

35. Ice-fishing Secret

Two men were out in the middle of a frozen lake, ice-fishing. They had been there, freezing, for two hours, without a bite.

A young boy came out and chopped a hole in the ice, just a few feet away from the men.

To their amazement, he dropped in his line, and, a few seconds later, pulled out a fish. Again, he put his fishing line into the water, and pulled out another fish.

"Charlie," said one of the men, "why don't you go over and ask the kid what his secret is for catching fish?"

Charlie walked over to the boy and asked, "Young man, what is your secret for catching fish?"

The boy replied, "Um a mum a mum aw a."

Charlie answered, "I couldn't understand you."

Again the boy said, "Um a mum a mum aw a."

Thinking the boy had a major speech impediment, he said, "I'm sorry, son. I still can't understand you."

With that, the lad spat into his hand, and said, "You gotta keep your worms warm."

36. 1930s Traveling Salesman's Adventures

During the Depression, a traveling salesman comes upon a farm house. It is growing dark, and he stops to ask for shelter for the night.

The farmer readily agrees, but states he'd have to sleep with his son.

"That's perfectly OK with me," the salesman replies. "I'm happy not to have to sleep in the barn."

"We're about to have supper. Would you join us?" asks the farmer's wife.

"I'd be delighted."

The salesman is introduced to the farmer's young son, and is impressed with the child's manners.

During dinner the boy is very polite, asking if the salesman wants more potatoes, or meat, or dessert?

Following dinner, the child says, "It's time for me to go to bed. Goodnight, mother. Goodnight, father. Goodnight, sir."

The salesman compliments the child's family, saying, "I've never met such a well-mannered child. I am very impressed with how you have brought him up. Now, I think I had better excuse myself and go to bed. I don't want to wake the boy. So, I'll say goodnight, too."

Opening the bedroom door, the salesman is struck by the beautiful scene. The child is on the far side of the bed, his hands folded in prayer. Not to appear un-Christian, the salesman kneels on his side of the bed, closes his eyes, and folds his hands in prayer.

After a few moments, he opens his eyes, and finds the child staring at him.

"Whatcha doin', mister?"

"I'm doing the same thing you are, son."

"Ma ain't gonna like that. The pot's on my side."

37. Clerical Friends

A Catholic Church and a Jewish Synagogue were on opposite corners of an intersection. The priest and rabbi became good friends, and were often seen walking together through the nearby woods, communing with nature.

One day, the priest asked the rabbi if he ever did anything against the tenets of his religion.

Thinking for a moment, the rabbi replied, "When I was young, I did eat ham once. As long as you brought it up, Father, have you ever done anything against the rules of your church?"

"When I was a young lad, before I took my vows, I did fornicate once."

They walked silently for awhile, and then the rabbi poked his elbow into the priest's side and chuckled, "Better than eating ham, wasn't it?"

38. Sex Expert

A noted sex-researcher was giving a lecture on the number of different positions couples use when having sex. "After extensive research of all cultures and religions from earliest written history, I can confidently state there are forty-seven positions for engaging in sex."

A man in the back of the room raised his hand.

"Yes, sir?" the lecturer queried.

The man replied, "There's forty-eight."

"I assure you, sir, there are only forty-seven. After I describe all of them, I would appreciate your informing me of the one I have missed."

With that, the expert launched into lecture. "Ladies and gentlemen, I will start with the missionary position. As you can see from the slide, this is where the man lies face down, in the prone position, above, and facing, the woman who is in the supine position."

From the back of the room a voice called out, "Forty-nine."

39. Martin Eye

A young nun, on a street corner at Christmastime, is soliciting funds for charity. A gentleman walks up to her and says, "Sister, you look very cold. Why don't you come into this bar and I'll buy you a drink."

She replies, "Oh, I don't think it would look right for me to go into a bar."

"Nonsense, Priests drink. There's no reason you shouldn't have a cocktail to warm your insides."

They go into a bar, and the man inquires, "What would you like to drink?"

"I've heard of a drink called a martin eye, with an olive."

"You mean a martini. I'll get you one."

At the bar, the bartender asks, "What can I get for you, sir?"

"I'll have a scotch, straight up, and a martin eye."

The bartender says, "Is that little nun in here again?"

40. Neophyte Parachutist

On his first jump, the young man is frozen in the hatch, tightly grasping the frame. "What if it doesn't open?" he queries the instructor.

"I've told you: the rip cord is tied to the static line. The moment you go out the door, it opens your chute."

"What if it doesn't open?"

"You've got your emergency chute on your chest. Just pull the handle and the chute will open."

"What if it doesn't open?"

"If all else fails, bank to the east, put your hands together, and shout, 'Buda, Buda, Buda.'"

"What good will that do?" asks the kid.

Exasperated, the instructor shoves the young man off the plane.

Sure enough, the main chute does not open. The young man pulls the handle of the emergency chute rip-cord, and ends up with the handle in his hand. Remembering the instructor's last words, he banks to the east and shouts, "Buda! Buda! Buda!"

A huge arm shoots out of a cloud, catches the young man in its hand, and gently sets him down on the ground.

The fellow steps off and says, "Thank God."

The arm comes up and **WHAM,** flattens him.

41. Savoir Faire

Three Frenchmen were trying to develop a situation which would define *savoir faire*.

The first man gave an example. "If a man comes home and opens the bedroom door and finds a man making love to his wife, and he quietly closes the door—*zat is savoir faire*."

"Non," said the second man. "If a man comes home and opens the bedroom door and finds his wife making love with another man, and says, 'Please, continue'—and closes the door—*zat is savoir faire'*."

"Non, non," said the third Frenchman. "If a man comes home and opens the bedroom door and finds a man making love to his wife, and says 'Please continue,' and the man does—*zat* is *savoir faire*."

42. Herpes

A Jewish man comes home from seeing his doctor.

His wife inquires, "What did the doctor say was your trouble?"

"He said I have herpes."

"What is that?"

"I don't know."

"Just a minute," his wife comments, "I'll look it up."

From the next room his wife shouts, "Papa, not to worry. It's a disease of the gentiles."

43. The Anniversary Present

On their fiftieth wedding anniversary, the husband asks his wife why she always charges him twenty dollars every time they have sex.

She replies, "Open the drapes."

Confused by her direction, he opens the drapes, and sees the twenty-story office building that has been across the street for several years. "OK, dear. I opened the drapes. What does that have to do with your charging me twenty dollars every time we made love?"

"What do you see?" she asks.

"I see that office building. What about it?"

"It's yours. Every time we made love, I invested the money. I bought the building for our fiftieth wedding anniversary."

"Sweetheart, why didn't you tell me? I would have given you all my business!"

Hospital visiting hours are from 8 AM to 4:30 PM.

44. American Indian Arrives at the Hyatt-Regency

A somewhat-decrepit old Indian walks into the Hyatt Hotel. His suitcase is tied with a rope; a red bandana is around his neck. At the front desk, he says, "Me want um room."

The clerk observes the Indian and decides the man is not the type of clientele they desire in the hotel. "Sir," he inquires, "do you have a reservation?"

"Me come from reservation. No got reservation."

"Sir," the clerk continues, hoping to dissuade the Indian, "the only room we have available is the Presidential Suite."

"How much is um?"

"Five hundred a night," states the clerk. To his amazement, the Indian pulls out a wad of hundred-dollar bills.

"Me take um five nights. Give um register."

The clerk complies, and the Indian meticulously makes an X.

Still trying to avoid having the Indian as a guest, the clerk remarks, "I'm sorry, sir. I forgot to tell you the room comes with a woman."

"How much is um?"

"Also, five hundred a night."

Me take um for five nights." He peels off more bills, and requests the register again.

The clerk turns the register around to the Indian who carefully draws a circle around his X.

"Why'd you do that, sir?"

"You run um whore house. Me use um assumed name."

45. Oral Roberts

Oral Roberts dies and goes to heaven.

St. Peter asks, "Your name?"

"Oral Roberts, sir."

St. Peter inquires, "THE Oral Roberts, the faith healer from Earth?"

"Yes, sir."

"Come with me," St. Peter directs. "I have someone who wants to meet you."

St. Pete brings Oral Roberts to Jesus. "Jesus, this is Oral Roberts."

"THE Oral Roberts, the faith healer from Earth?"

"Yes, sir," Oral responds.

"Come with me, I have someone who wants to meet you."

Jesus takes Oral Roberts to God.

"God," Jesus pronounces, "this is Oral Roberts."

"THE Oral Roberts, the faith healer from Earth?"

"Yes, sir."

God leans forward and says, "I've been having this pain in my left shoulder . . ."

46. Timbuktu

Two men die and arrive at the Pearly Gates together. St. Peter inquires as to their profession while on earth.

"Engineers," both reply.

"Oh, gee," moans St. Peter. "We've got too many engineers up here, and they are so boring. For all of eternity, they only talk technical subjects and mathematical formulas. I've decided you'll have to display some capabilities, other than science, to get into Heaven. Otherwise, I will have to assign you to Purgatory. As a test of your abilities in areas other than science and mathematics, I want you to construct a poem around the word Timbuktu."

The first man thinks for a while and recites, "As I walked along the sandy shore and listened to the ocean's roar. I saw a ship a-sailing, on that ocean blue: destination Timbuktu."

"Excellent!" St. Peter exclaims. "You will be a good asset." He turns to the second man and asks, "Have you composed a poem?"

"Yep," he replied. "Tim and I a-hunting went. We spied three girls within a tent.

They were three, and we were two. So I bucked one, and Tim bucked two."

47. Three Trained Dogs

(When I first heard this joke, the engineer's dog's name was slide-rule)

An attorney, a medical doctor, and an engineer were good friends who were always bragging about their trained dogs. One day they decided to meet at the park, and display their dogs' capabilities.

The engineer led off. "Computer," he called to his dog. "Do your thing."

The dog dragged a sack of bones in front of the group, and arrayed them into a replica of the State Capital. That proved the dog had a good sense of architecture, and was well trained.

The doctor called his dog, "Hey, Stethoscope. Do your thing."

The dog promptly brought out a bag of bones, dumped them on the ground, and arranged them into a human skeleton. This proved the dog had a good sense of anatomy, and was well trained.

The attorney then called to his dog, "Hey, Shyster. Do your thing."

Shyster screwed both dogs and stole their bones. This proved he had learned well from his master.

48. American in Belfast

An American walked down a street in Belfast one night, when a man stepped out of the shadows, stuck a gun into the American's side, and whispered, "What's your religion?"

The American thought for a second. *If I say I'm Catholic, I could be shot. If I say I'm Protestant, I could be shot.* So he replied to the man, "I'm Jewish."

The voice said, "I must be the luckiest Arab in Ireland."

49. Church Bells

An old man from Pennsylvania was telling his friend O'Malley that he was able to tell from the sound of a church's bell which church was summoning its members to services on Sunday mornings. He said, "Each bell takes on the nationality of its parishioners. For instance, when I hear the Lithuanian Catholic Church bell ring out with, 'Aye yon ko, Aye yon ko, Aye yon ko,' I know it's the Lithuanian church. When I hear 'Po lan der, Po lan der, Po lan der,' I know it is the Polish Catholic Church calling its congregation.

"But my faith in a forgiving God is always restored when I hear the Irish Catholic Church bell calling the Irish Catholics to church with its resounding 'Bum, Bum, Bum.'"

50. Naming Indian Babies

A young Indian boy asked his father, "Father, how do you choose names for Indian children?"

"In our tribe, after the baby is born, the tent flap is opened; and the first thing a mother sees is the name given to the child. For instance, when your sister was born, your mother saw the moon rising. So your sister was named Rising Moon. When your brother was born, your mother saw a bear running on the ridge, so he is named Running Bear. What makes you ask, Two Dogs Humping?"

51. Boy and Girl Statues

In Lincoln Park, there were two statues: one of a teen-age boy, and the other, a teen-age girl. They had been in the park, facing each other, for a hundred years. One day, the God of statues came along. He whispered in the boy statue's ear, "You have been a wonderful statue for all these years. You've given great pleasure to all who have come here. I'm granting you one hour of life."

The God of statues went to the girl statue, and whispered the same message in her ear.

The boy statue looked at the girl statue: she laughed, and they both jumped down off their pedestals and disappeared into the bushes. There were great shrieks of laughter, and rustling of the bushes. Finally the two emerged, looking very disheveled, flushed, and a bit breathless. The girl asked the boy, "Do you want to do it again?"

"Yes," he chuckled. "Only this time, you hold the pigeons while I poop on them."

52. Charades

Two men had a friendly rivalry challenging each other in games of charades. However, John was usually a better guesser than Bob. One day, Bob had an inspiration, so he challenged John to a game that night.

When John arrived, Bob called "Come out. girls." Out trooped seven nude women. "Line up facing the wall," he instructed. "Now, numbers two and four face forward."

"OK, John. What is it?"

John studied the girls for a moment then laughed derisively. "That's easy. *The William Tell Overture.* Rump, titty, rump, titty, rump, rump, rump."

53. Misunderstanding

A doctor and his wife go to a restaurant featuring dinner and dancing. As they sit down, the doctor sees one of his elderly patients jitterbugging with a lovely young woman.

When the music ends, the couples leave the dance floor, and are passing the table when the man recognizes the doctor. "Doc," he said, "that was the best advice you ever gave me. I feel great."

"What advice was that?"

"You told me to be cheerful and get a hot mama."

"You misunderstood me. I said you should be careful—you've got a heart murmur."

54. Boasters

Three men, who graduated from the same high school, accidentally meet at the corner of Hollywood and Vine in Los Angeles.

After shaking hands, one asks another, "What've you been doing the past ten years since we graduated?"

The man replies, "I'm in the medical profession. Have you ever heard of pennicilium? I was on the team that discovered it."

"My, what a coincidence," the first responds. "I happen to be in the same profession myself. Have you heard of the *Saukey* vaccine? I was on Doctor Salkey's team that invented it."

They turn to the third man, and ask what he's been doing.

"Well, gentlemen, strange as it may seem, I'm sort of in the same profession."

"Wait a minute," says the first fellow. "Two of us in the medical profession are a coincidence; three is impossible."

"No," the third man stated. "Have you heard of gonorrhea?"

"Don't tell us you invented that!"

"Nope, I'm sort of the west coast distributor."

55. Mystery

Question: What goes clip, clop, clip, clop, bang, bang, clippity clop, clippity clop?

Answer: An Amish drive-by shooting.

56. Salvation Army Worker

A snow storm necessitates a traveling salesman having to stay at a hotel during the Christmas season. On his way up to his room, he asks the bellhop, "Do you think you could find me a woman for the night?"

The bellhop replies that he'll try, but it might be difficult so close to Christmas.

The salesman is emptying his suitcase and putting the clothes away when there is a knock on the door. Opening it, he sees a woman in a Salvation Army uniform, standing in the hall.

"What can I do for you?" he asks.

"You asked for a woman, didn't you?"

"Yes, please come in. I'll be with you when I finish putting my clothes away."

When he finishes and turns around, the woman remarks, "Is that a wedding ring on your finger?"

"Yes." he replied. "What about it?"

The woman indignantly stomps from the room, declaring, "We serve the needy, not the greedy."

57. Your Weight and Fortune: Twenty-five Cents

A nun is seated in the waiting area at the Los Angeles Airport, waiting for her plane. She spies a weighing scale advertising "Your weight and fortune: twenty-five cents." Intrigued, she walks over, stands on the scale, and inserts a quarter. Out comes a card reading: "You weigh 125 pounds; you're a nun; and you're going to Chicago."

She takes her seat, thinking about the correctness of the fortune. She could see no one who could have programmed the scale to provide such accurate information. Curiosity compels her to try the scale again to see if the same fortune is repeated.

Again, she steps on the scale, inserts a quarter, and out comes another card. It reads: "You weigh 125 pounds; you're a nun; you're going to Chicago; and you're going to play the violin."

She sits down and contemplates the new fortune. *That's stupid. I've never played a violin in my life.* Just then a cowboy walks up to her and asks, "Sister, would you mind watching my fiddle while I go to the men's room?"

"Of course not, would you mind if I played it?"

"Nope, you go right ahead."

The nun opens the case, takes out the violin, tucks it under her chin, and plays a lively little tune. The other waiting passengers applaud her effort. Embarrassed, she puts the violin back in its case, just as the cowboy returns.

This is too much for her to comprehend. The fortune was right; she played a violin, never having had a lesson. *What else would the fortune-telling scale predict?* She can't resist another fortune, and so goes back to the machine.

After she inserts the quarter, out pops the card. This time it reads: "You weigh 125 pounds; you're a nun; you're going to Chicago; you've played the violin. Now you're going to pass gas."

That's impossible. I would never do such a thing in a crowd. She steps off the scale, loses her balance, grabs the machine for support, and lets out a loud fart. Mortified by her indiscretion, she hurries to her seat. Still, that machine seems to force her to find out her latest fortune.

She inserts another quarter, and snatches the card. It states: "You weigh 125 pounds; you're a nun; you're not going to Chicago; you fiddled and farted around, and missed your plane."

58. Dumb Blonde Joke #23

A redhead, a brunette and a blonde are castaways on a deserted island. One day as they walk along the shore, they come upon a bottle.

After they uncork it, out pops a genie.

"I can only grant three wishes for rescuing me from my imprisonment." Turning to the brunette, he asks, "What is your wish?"

She replies, "I have been on this island for five years. I miss my husband and children. I wish to return home."

Whoosh. She is gone.

He then asks the redhead, "What is your wish?"

She, too, asks to be returned to her family, and disappears in an instant.

Addressing the blonde, he asks, "What is your wish?"

"I'm so lonely. I wish my friends were back with me."

59. Second Thoughts

A doctor and his wife are attending a convention dinner when she inquires, "Who's that beautiful woman with Doctor Bob?"

"That's his mistress."

"That's disgusting. Mary ought to divorce him."

"Well," says her husband, "see that redhead standing over there?"

"Yes, she's beautiful."

"That's my mistress, dear."

"You beast! I've never been so insulted in my life. How dare you flaunt your mistress at me? I'm going to see our lawyer in the morning, and get a divorce."

"Don't be too hasty," her husband cautions. "Remember, I make $500,000 a year; we've got two children, one in college; we have three homes: one in New York, one in the Catskills and one on the French Riviera; you drive a Mercedes convertible; and we've got servants, so you don't have to do any work. You might get half of everything, but now you have it all."

His wife looks up at him and says, "Ours is prettier than theirs."

60. Seaman's Confession

Two seamen are about to embark on a weekend liberty, when one says to the other, "Wait a few minutes; I have to go to confession."

Once in the confessional, the seaman says, "Father, I have sinned."

The priest asks, "What sin have you committed for which you desire forgiveness and absolution, Mulvaney?"

"I committed adultery, Father."

"Who was the woman, Michael?"

"I'm sorry, Father; I can't give you her name."

"Mulvaney," the priest says sternly, "I can't give you absolution unless I know her name."

"I'm sorry, Father: I just can't."

"Tell me; was it Jennie O'Brian, the Base Exchange manager's wife?"

"No, Father; I will not tell you."

"Was it Mary Jones, Commander Smith's secretary?"

"Father, I will not tell you."

"Then get out of here. There's no absolution for you."

Outside, Mick's buddy asks, "Did you get absolution?"

"No, but I got a couple of good leads."

61. Snow on the Roof, but Fire in the Furnace

A seventy-five-year-old man, asked to what he attributes his old age, says, "My father."

"How old was your father when he died?"

"Who said he was dead? He's ninety-five."

"Do you know what he credits for his age?"

"I guess it would be grandpa, his father."

"How old was your grandfather when he died?"

"Who said he's dead? He's one hundred-fifteen. In fact, he's getting married next week."

"Why does he want to get married?"

"Who says he wants to?"

62. Seven-day Camel

An archeologist is searching for a camel that can travel to an oasis seven days distant. Every camel dealer can only provide camels capable of traveling five days without water. Finally, he comes upon Abdul, the used camel dealer.

"Sir," he asks, "I have need of a camel capable of going seven days without water. Do you have such an animal?"

"Of course, come with me, and I will sell you a seven-day camel."

They walk over to his herd and pick out a camel. "First, he must drink," says Abdul. He leads the beast to a watering trough, and it lowers its head to the water. After slurping the water for ten minutes, the camel raises its head and belches.

Abdul says, "Now he is a five-day camel. When I say 'now', you push the camel's head into the water and hold it there." Abdul steps behind the camel and yells, "Now!"

The archeologist pushes the camel's head into the water. Abdul picks up two flat rocks and slams the camel's testicles between the rocks. The camel goes, "OOOOOOOH," and raises its head from the water.

"Now he's a seven-day camel."

"Doesn't that hurt?" queries the archeologist.

"Only if I smash my finger between the rocks."

63. Talcum Powder

A man calls to his wife, "Honey, I'm going out to get a pack of cigarettes."

"It's pretty late. Are you sure the market is open?'

"They stay open until midnight."

"OK. Don't be gone too long."

He goes to the market and buys the cigarettes. On the way home, he passes a bar and decides to have a drink. As he's nursing his drink, a lovely woman comes in and sits down beside him.

They were having a conversation, when she asks, "Would you like to come to my apartment? It's right around the corner."

He agrees, and, after some lovemaking, he glances at his watch. It is two o'clock.

"Quick," he asks. "Do you have any talcum powder?"

"What do you want talcum powder for?" she replies.

"No time to explain," he responds in a panicked voice.

The woman brings the powder and he dusts his hands, and then dashes home.

There is his wife at the door, visibly disturbed. "Where have you been for three hours?"

"Honey, this is the truth. I bought the cigarettes, stopped at the bar for a drink, met this woman; we went up to her apartment and made love. I saw what time it was and came right home."

"Let me see your hands," she demands.

He showed her his hands.

"Liar!" she screamed. "Ya bum—you went bowling again."

64. God Creates Adam and Eve

After God created Adam, He summoned him to his office.

"Yes, God, you called?"

"Yes, Adam, I want you to go down the valley."

"What's a valley?"

God explained, and Adam was satisfied.

God went on. "Then, I want you to cross the river."

"What's a river?"

God explained, and Adam understood.

"Adam, then I want you to go up the hill."

Before Adam could interrupt, God explained what a hill was. God continued, "Adam, you will find a cave."

"What's a cave?"

God, not fast enough, explains what a cave is.

Next, God says, "I want you to go into the cave and meet the woman, Eve."

"What's a woman, Eve?" Adam questioned.

God explained what a woman was. Adam was very interested.

Then, God continued, "I want you two to multiply."

"What's multiply?"

God was beginning to think He'd made a mistake in creating this dumbbell. But explained what He meant by multiply.

Adam was very intrigued by the description, so he went down the valley, across the river, up the hill, into the cave, and met Eve.

Shortly, Adam came out of the cave, went down the hill, across the river, and up the valley to stand before God.

God looked up and asked, "Now what?"

Adam looked at God and asked, "What's a headache?"

65. Grounds for Divorce

A woman walks into an attorney's office and announces, "I wants a divorce."

The attorney asks, "Do you have grounds?"

"Yep, we've got about eighty acres."

"No," he replies, "I meant do you have a suit?"

"No, he has a suit, I have a dress."

A little exasperated, he tries to clarify, "Do you have a case?"

"Nope, we has a John Deere."

Getting more irritated by the second, the attorney asks, "Do you have a grudge?"

"Sure," she replied. "That's where we park our John Deere."

Totally exasperated, he asks, "Lady, why do you want a divorce?"

"Lack of communication!"

66. Texas Department of Water and Power

A rancher is unsaddling his horse when an official State vehicle drives in and parks nearby. A man gets out and announces, "I'm with the Texas Department of Water and Power, and I'm here to test all the water supplies on your ranch."

The rancher replied, "Go ahead, but stay out of that field over there."

The man takes out his wallet and extracts a card. He shows it to the rancher, saying, "This card says I can go anywhere I please, and at any time I please. No questions asked or answered. Is that clear?"

The rancher leads his horse into the barn and declares, "Yep. You go anywhere you please, any time you please."

Of course, the officious official goes directly to the field he was warned about.

The rancher puts his horse into its stall, and walks out of the barn. Then he hears the official screaming. Turning toward the sound he sees the man running as fast as he can for the fence, with a very angry bull at his heels, gaining at each step. "Help me," cries the official.

The rancher cups his hands to his lips, like a megaphone, and yells, "Show him the card. Show him the card."

67. Talking Dog

A fellow is driving through the hills of Arkansas when he notices a sign on the fence of an old shack, reading: "Talking Dog for Sale."

It intrigues him, so he stops and goes up to the door. A man answers, "What do you want, stranger?"

"I came to see the talking dog."

"He's around back."

The man goes to the backyard and sees a dog tied up to a dog house. "Are you the talking dog?"

"Yes, I am. What can I do for you?"

Suspicious, the man looks around for a speaker. "Can you really talk?" he asks.

"Yes. You won't find any wires or speakers hidden here. They're so backward they wouldn't know what one looked like."

"When did you find out you could talk?"

"I was just a puppy when I learned I had this skill. When I was a year old, I applied to the CIA for a job as a spy, and they hired me on the spot. I worked for them for six years, listening in on secret meetings and infiltrating spy cells. Finally I got tired of jetting around and applied for a job with Homeland Security. I spent three years in airports, and was responsible for thwarting numerous attempts to sabotage commercial planes."

"How did you end up here?"

"I'm getting too old, so I thought I'd retire. Unfortunately, these hillbillies captured me and have kept me chained to this doghouse."

"I'll be right back, dog. I'm going to buy you and take you to my country home, where you'll be free to go anywhere you please."

The man walks to the front of the building and asks the owner, "How much for the dog?"

"Twenty bucks," the redneck says.

"How come you're selling a talking dog so cheap?"

"Cause he's a liar. He ain't done none of them things!"

68. Counting

A woman is walking past a mental hospital, when she hears a large group chanting, "37, 37, 37, 37," behind a wooden fence.

Unable to overcome her curiosity, she finds a knothole in the fence. Pressing her face against the fence, she peers through the hole, and receives a poke in the eye.

The chanting continues: "38, 38, 38 . . ."

69. Speed Limits

A motorcycle cop is hiding behind a billboard along Interstate 15. He is astounded to see a Cadillac, filled with women, traveling at fifteen miles an hour. He races out from behind the billboard and waves the driver to pull off the road. Looking in the car, he sees all the women are ashen-faced and trembling.

The officer parks his motorcycle behind the Cadillac and walks up to the window. The woman driver inquires, "What's wrong, officer?"

"Ma'am," he replies, "why are you going fifteen miles an hour on the freeway?"

"Well, officer, I was just following the speed limit. The sign says 15."

"Ma'am, that's the number of the highway, not the speed limit."

"I'm sorry, officer. I won't make that mistake again."

"I hope I didn't scare you ladies—you look frightened."

"It wasn't you, officer. We just came off Highway 122."

70. Clairvoyant

Two men are in the airport's men's room, standing at the urinals. One looks at the other and remarks, "You're Jewish."

The second man turns his head to look at the man, and replies, "Yeah, so what?"

The first guy says, "You're from New York."

The other second replies, "We just got off the plane from New York, so what?"

The first man grins and states, "You live somewhere between 126th and 150th."

The second man answers, with surprise in his voice, "You're right again."

The first continues, "I'll bet you attend temple Beth Al."

"Holy smoke!" exclaims the second man. "How'd you know that?"

"Rabinowitz cuts on the bias, and you're peeing on my shoe."

71. Lunar Excursion Module Astronauts

Two astronauts are walking on the lunar surface away from the Excursion Module, when one asks the other, "Have you got the key?"

The other astronaut replies, "Key? I thought you had the key!"

72. Where's God?

Two young boys, 9 and 11, were extremely mischievous. They had a reputation for always getting into trouble, playing pranks on the townspeople. If any mischief occurred in town, the two boys were usually involved. Their parents were unable to curb the children's behavior. The boys' mother heard that a preacher in town had been successful in disciplining children, and asked him to speak to the boys.

The preacher asked to see them individually, so the mother sent the younger to see the preacher in the morning. The older boy had an afternoon appointment.

The preacher, a big man with a booming voice, has the boy sit in a chair in front of the desk. He asks him sternly, "Son, do you know where God is?"

The boy shivers in his chair at the red-faced preacher, and makes no response.

The preacher raises his voice; his face becomes more flushed, and he repeats the question: "Where is God?"

The boy cowers in the chair and makes no attempt to answer.

The preacher raises his hand, points to the boy, and bellows, "Where is God?"

The kid screams, dashes out of the room, runs directly home, and dives into his closet, slamming the door behind him.

When his older brother hears him come home crying and run into his closet, he opens the closet door and asks, "What's wrong?"

"We're in big trouble! God is missing, and they think we did it!"

73. Penance

(Best told using names familiar to the audience.)

Jim Jones dies and goes to heaven. While walking down a path with St. Peter, he sees his friend, Tim Tyler, shackled to a homely woman. "Why is Tim tied to such an unattractive woman?"

St. Peter responds, "In his youth, Tim led a pretty bad life. This is his penance, being tied to a homely woman for eternity."

They go further along the path and come upon his friend Bob chained to a very ugly woman. Quick on the uptake, Jim says, "I guess Bob was really bad, to be tied to such a grotesque woman."

"You're right," answered St. Peter.

Turning a corner he spies his pal Bill shackled to Bo Derek. "Gosh, Bill must have been very good to be tied to Bo Derek."

"Nope," said St. Peter. "Bo was very, very bad."

74. Draftee

A young draftee is being interviewed by the Army psychiatrist. "Son, what would you do if you saw an enemy soldier in front of you?"

"I'd shoot him with my gun."

"What if your gun jammed?"

"I'd stick him with my bayonet."

"What if it broke?"

"I'd cut off my left arm and beat him to death with it."

"That's crazy," says the doctor.

The draftee replies, "Write that down."

75. The Nude Runner

A woman is having a daytime affair while her husband is at work. One rainy day she's in bed with her boyfriend when, to her horror, she hears her husband's car pull into the driveway.

"Oh, my God!" she exclaims. "Hurry, grab your clothes and jump out of the window, my husband's home early."

"I can't jump out the window. It's raining out there," he replies.

"If my husband catches us in here, he'll kill us both. He's got a hot temper and carries a gun, so the rain is the least of your problems."

The boyfriend grabs his clothes and jumps out the window. As he runs down the street in the rain, he quickly discovers he has run right into the middle of the town's annual marathon, so he starts running beside the others. Being naked, with his clothes tucked under his arm, he tries to blend in as well as he can.

After a little while a small group of runners who've been watching him with some curiosity, jogs closer.

"Do you always run in the nude?" one asks.

"Oh, yes," he replies. "It feels so wonderfully free."

Another runner moves alongside. "Do you always run carrying your clothes with you under your arm?"

"Oh, yes," the nude man declares, breathlessly. "That way I can get dressed right at the end of the run, and get in my car to go home."

Then a third runner casts his eyes a little lower and asks, "Do you always wear a condom when you run?"

"Nope," the lover replies. "Only when it's raining."

76. Murphy's Apartment Building

Murphy owned a six-flat apartment in a neighborhood that was experiencing an influx of Jewish families.

Over the years, the tenants tried to convince Murphy to sell the apartment building to them. He always refused.

Mr. Goldberg said to his wife, "Sadie, you get along very well with Mr. Murphy. Why don't you try to find out why he won't sell the building to us? We've offered him a very good price."

Sadie went to Murphy's apartment, and an hour later she came back, all excited. "Papa," she said breathlessly, "I know why Mr. Murphy will not sell the building to us."

"Why?" he coaxed.

"Mr. Murphy says he's made love to every woman in the building but one, and when he makes it with her, he'll sell."

"And we know who that woman is, don't we, Sadie?"

"Yes, it's probably that stingy Mrs. Nussbaum who lives on the third floor."

77. Possibly

"Students," the teacher began, "today our new word is 'possibly.' Can anyone give me a sentence using the word possibly?"

Jane raised her hand. "Yes, Jane. Do you have a sentence using the word?"

"Yesterday, I saw a man with a fishing pole walking toward the lake. Possibly, he was going fishing."

"Excellent, Jane, does anyone else have an example? Billy?"

"Yes, Miss Jones. I saw a man with a baseball walking with a boy with a baseball bat. Possibly, they were going to play baseball."

"Very good, Billy." Just then Tyler raised his hand. The teacher was reluctant to call on him because he had a perverse sense of humor, often embarrassing her and the class. "OK, Tyler. What's your sentence?"

"Yesterday I saw Daddy standing by the piano with his pants down, and the maid with her dress up. Possibly they were going to pee on the piano."

78. Showing Off to the Wife

John was addressing the ball on the ninth tee when his partner said, "Come on, John, hit the damn ball."

"Give me time. This has to be a special shot."

"What's so special about this shot?"

"See that woman standing by the dining room?"

"Yeah," replied Tom. "What about her?"

"That's my wife."

"My God, man, she's 400 yards away. You can't possibly hit her from here."

79. Is Hell Exothermic or Endothermic?

A professor of thermodynamics posed the following question to his class: "Is Hell exothermic or endothermic? Show proof."

One student proposed the following answer:

First, we must postulate whether souls have mass. We must assume that souls have mass. If souls have no mass, the addition or subtraction of souls would not increase or decrease the temperature of Hell.

Next, we must determine the rate of increase or decrease in the number of souls entering and leaving Hell. Obviously, when a soul enters Hell, it never leaves. Then, we must determine the rate of souls entering Hell. Every religion believes all those of different religions are going to Hell. Since a person is not a member of more than one religion, we can predict that everyone is going to Hell. An analysis of birth and death rates conclusively proves that the number of souls going to Hell is increasing exponentially.

Next, we must determine the rate of change in the volume of Hell. Boyle's Law states: in order for the temperature and pressure of Hell to remain constant, the ratio of the mass of the souls entering Hell, compared to its volume, must remain constant.

Answer 1: If the volume of Hell is expanding at a slower rate than the number of souls entering, the temperature and pressure would increase until all Hell breaks loose.

Answer 2: If the volume of Hell is expanding faster than the mass of souls entering Hell, the temperature would decrease until Hell freezes over.

So which is it? As no one has ever returned from Hell to provide such information, we must determine the answer using some sort of empirical evidence.

If the postulate "I'll sleep with you when Hell freezes over," given me by Miss Cynthia Jones during our freshman year is accurate, and adding the fact that we spent last night together, I must assume Answer 2 is correct.

80. The Hated Outhouse

A young farm boy hated the outhouse his family used. It smelled terrible during the summer, and he froze his butt off in it during the winter. One day there was a horrific rain storm, and the creek next to the outhouse became a roaring river. As the water crept ever closer to the outhouse, the boy seized the opportunity.

Using a tree branch, he pried up the outhouse until it toppled into the water, and then he watched it disappear downstream.

That evening, the farmer brought a switch into the house. "Son, did you tip the outhouse into the creek?"

"Yes, father, I did it."

"Well, son, you're going to get a whipping for doing it."

"But father, when George Washington told the truth and admitted he cut down the cherry tree, his father forgave him."

"I know that. However, I'll bet George's father was not in the cherry tree."

81. The Duffer

A golfer was addressing his ball, concentrating on the direction his ball was to take, when the loudspeaker in the starter's shack bellowed, "Will the gentleman on the ladies' tee please bring his ball back to the men's tee?"

The golfer continued his practice swing, and determined the trajectory of his ball. Again the loudspeaker voice reiterated, "Will the man on the first tee please bring his ball back and use the men's tee?"

The golfer turned around and yelled, "Will you please be quiet while I take my second shot?"

82. The Chinese Newlyweds

On their wedding night, the young Chinese man, attempting to present himself to be sexually knowledgeable, said to his bride,

"My darring, I know this you first time. I be very gentle. I do what you want. Just ret me know what you want."

His bride giggled and replied, "My friends say I should ask for 69."

The poor man had no idea what 69 meant. He thought for a minute, and said, incredulously, "You want cashew chicken and steamed vegetables?"

83. The Prescription

A woman walked up to the pharmacist and said, "I want some arsenic."

The pharmacist asked, "What do you want to do with the arsenic?"

"I want to kill my husband."

"Madam, I can't sell you arsenic to kill your husband. I'd lose my license and you'd go to jail."

The woman pulled a picture from her purse and handed it to the pharmacist. It showed her husband making love to the pharmacist's wife.

"That's different," he said. "I didn't know you had a prescription."

84. Washer Repairman

A woman called a washer repairman. There was no answer, so she left her name and address, told him she had to go to work, and that the key was under the floor mat. She gave him the following instructions: "Don't worry about my dog; he's big and will just watch you work. However, do not, under any circumstances, talk to the parrot."

The repairman entered the home and was confronted by a vicious-looking Doberman, who lay down and watched him as he worked. The parrot was another matter. It kept up a continuous, one-sided conversation, describing the repairman's family heritage, ugly looks, incompetence, and stupidity.

Finally, the man could stand it no longer. "Shut up, you damn bird; I'll strangle you if you say another word."

The parrot said, "Sic him, Rex!"

85. Don't Mess with Seniors

A woman went to breakfast at a restaurant where the senior special was two eggs, two strips of bacon, hash browns, and toast, for $1.99.

"Those sounds good," she said to the waitress, "but hold the eggs."

"Then I'll have to charge you $2.49," the girl replied. "Because you're ordering *a la carte*."

"You mean I have to pay more for not ordering the eggs?" the woman asked incredulously.

"Yes," replied the waitress.

"OK, then, I'll take the special."

"How do you want the eggs?" asked the waitress.

"Raw and in the shell," the woman answered.

86. At the Olympics Without Tickets

An Englishman, a Scotsman and an Irishman were in Sydney on business during the Summer Olympics. Unfortunately, they were unable to get tickets.

The Englishman had an idea. He walked across the street to a clothesline stretched between two metal posts. He removed the pole supporting the line, then walked to the entrance of the event. "Simpson, England, pole vault," he said to the guard, and walked through the gate.

Not to be outdone, the Scotsman picked up a manhole cover, tucked it under his arm, and said to the attendant, "MacTavish, Scotland, discus," and walked through the gate.

The Irishman couldn't let his friends outwit him, so he went back to a barrier and picked a coil of barbed wire, put it over his shoulder, and walked to the gate. He said to the guard, "Murphy, Ireland, fencing."

87. The Kissing Nun

A nun hailed a cab, and then gave the driver the name of a hotel as the destination. As they were cruising along, the nun noticed the driver kept looking at her in his rear view mirror.

"Young man, why do you keep looking at me?"

"To tell the truth, I'm ashamed to say, I've always wondered what it would be like to kiss a nun."

"Is that all? Pull over to that dark street and stop under the tree."

The driver complied.

"Now get into the back seat with me."

The driver opened his door and entered the rear seat.

The nun threw her arms around him and gave him the most passionate kiss he had ever had.

"I hope that satisfies your curiosity. Now, drive me to the hotel."

When they arrived, the chagrinned driver said, "I'm sorry for what I did, Sister. Please forgive me."

"No problem," the nun replied. "My name's Jack and I'm going to a masquerade ball."

88. The Golf Genie

A man took his wife to play her first game of golf; on her first drive she shanked the ball, and drove it through the window of a large home adjacent to the golf course. "Well," he said, "we'd better go over and see what your bad shot will cost us."

They knocked on the door, and a voice said, "Come on in."

When they entered, the damage the errant golf ball had caused was evident. There was glass everywhere and an antique bottle lay broken on the floor. A distinguished—looking man was reclining in an overstuffed chair. "We're so very sorry to have caused so much damage; we'll gladly pay for it."

"There is no need. You freed me from that bottle where I've been a prisoner for many years. For freeing me, I can offer you three wishes. However, I will grant each of you a wish, and save one for myself."

"Wow, that's great," the husband said. "I wish for a million dollars a year for the rest of my life."

"Done," said the genie. "It's the least I can do for you for freeing me from that bottle. I'll guarantee you a long and happy life." Turning to the wife, he asked, "What do you wish for, pretty lady?"

"I wish for beautiful homes in California, the Italian Riviera, and Barbados, with plenty of servants to take care of all our needs."

"Your wish is granted."

"Now, Genie," they both inquired. "What is your wish?"

"Since I've been trapped in that bottle for two hundred years, and without a woman, I wish to make love to your wife."

The request caught them by surprise. The husband looked at the wife and said, "He's given us all that money and three houses. What do you think, dearest?"

The wife thought it over and said, "Genie, I think it is only fair for the good fortune you've given us. If it's all right with you, honey, I'll have sex with him."

"You know I love you, honey. I'd do it for you."

The genie and the woman went upstairs to the bedroom, and made passionate love the rest of the afternoon. The genie had the stamina of a lion and was nearly insatiable. Finally he rolled over and spoke to the wife. "How old are you and your husband?"

"We're both 40," she said breathlessly.

"Imagine, you're both 40 years old and you both still believe in genies."

89. It's All in the Approach

Two buddies were drinking at a bar one night, when one turns to the other and says, "I don't know what to do. When I come home late after drinking a few beers, I turn off the car's engine and coast into the driveway. I take off my shoes, quietly unlock the door, tip-toe up the stairs into the bathroom, take off my clothes, and try to slip into the bed. My wife is always awake, and bawls me out for being so late."

His friend observes, "You're doing it all wrong. I come home, screech the brakes, slam the garage door, pound up the stairs, strip in the bedroom, pat my wife on the ass, and ask if she's ready for a little sex. She always pretends to be asleep. I never get a word out of her."

90. Best Bar in the World

An Italian, a Scotsman and an Irishman are in a bar, having a good time. They all agree this bar is very nice and a pleasant place to meet with friends.

The Scotsman remarked, "Aye, 'tis a fine place, but we have a bar in Glasgow that's better. In MacDougall's, you buy two drinks, and MacDougall buys the third drink."

"That's a-pretty good," said the Italian. "But in Napoli, we've got a place called 'Ronzoni's' where you buy a drink and Ronzoni buys a drink. You buy another drink, Ronzoni buys another."

They all agree it sounds like a great bar, but the Irishman says, "Where I come from, there's a bar called Murphy's in Dublin, where you buy the first drink, and they buy the next two drinks, then they take you in the back room, and get you laid."

"Wow," say the other two. "That's fantastic. Did that actually happen to you?"

"Nope, but it happened to my sister."

91. Keeping the Wife Happy

An elderly man and his wife had been invited to dinner with an equally old couple. Following dinner, he and the husband sat in the living room while the wives put the dishes in the dishwasher.

"How long have you and your wife been married?" the guest inquired.

"Fifty-nine years."

"No wonder you've been married so long. You always speak to her in such endearing terms; it's honey this, and darling that, or sweetie or dearest, all the time."

The husband replied, "I have to. I forgot her name ten years ago."

92. Inquisitive Daughter

"Mommy, how old are you?" the little girl asked her one morning at breakfast.

"Honey, it's not polite to ask a woman her age."

"Well then, how much do you weigh?"

"You should never ask a woman to reveal her weight."

"Mommy, why did you and daddy get a divorce?"

"What's with all these questions, young lady? I don't want to talk about your daddy and me. It hurts too much."

The little girl was disappointed and asked one of her friends why her mother didn't want her to know these things.

The friend replied, "I don't know why mothers won't tell these things to their own daughters, but I know how to get the answers."

"How?" the little girl asked.

"Just look on her driver's license. It's got all the answers."

That night the daughter looked at her mother's license. The next morning she proudly announced, "I know how old you are. You're 32, and you weigh 118 pounds."

"How did you find out, young lady?"

"I also know why you and daddy got a divorce."

"Why?"

"You got an F in sex."

93. Physiology Lesson

It takes your food seven seconds to get from your mouth to your stomach.

One human hair can support 3 kg (6.6 pounds).

The average man's penis is three times the length of his thumb.

Healthy human thigh bones are stronger than concrete.

A woman's heart beats faster than a man's.

There are about one trillion bacteria on each of your feet.

Women blink twice as fast as men.

The average person's skin weighs twice as much as the brain.

Your body uses 300 muscles to balance itself when you are standing still.

If saliva can't dissolve something, you cannot taste it.

Women reading this will be finished now.

Men are still checking their thumbs.

94. The Funeral Procession

A woman was seated on the patio of a coffee house in New Orleans when a strange funeral procession came down the street; it consisted of two hearses followed by a woman in black with a Doberman pinscher at her side, followed by a long line of women. Curious, she approached the woman in black and asked, "I'm sorry to intrude upon the funeral, but could you tell me who's in the hearses?"

The woman responded, "My husband is in the first, and my mother-in-law in the second."

"What happened to them?"

"My dog attacked my husband, and when his mother tried to stop him, he killed her, too."

"Could you loan me your dog?"

"Get in line."

95. The Date

A woman in a retirement community called her friend Irma for advice. "Irma, the new resident, Bill Thomas, asked me out on a date. You went out with him. What can you tell me about him?"

"Jean, he took me to dinner and the theater. He arrived on time, dressed in a tuxedo. He helped me on with my coat, and opened the door to the limousine he had chartered. The dinner was lovely, and he was a true gentleman all evening, making sure I was comfortable in the box he had reserved at the theater.

"When he walked me to my apartment, I asked him to come in. From that moment on, he was a sex-crazed beast. He ripped my new dress off, tore off my underwear, and made love to me for two hours."

"You're saying I should refuse to date him?"

"No! I'm saying wear an old dress."

96. Sex-training Kit

The morning after the first night of their honeymoon, the newlywed man said, "Honey, you were fantastic. You must have had experience with other men to have such sexy moves."

"No, dear, you are the only man I've ever made love to."

"Honey, it's OK to tell me the truth. I don't mind. You've had to have had experience to make such movements."

"Oh, no, I owe it to my do-it-yourself sex-training kit."

"I just can't believe you're so expert from a sex-training kit."

"Let me show you, dearest." She went into the closet and brought out a belt which she strapped to her waist. On the left and right, at the curve of her hips, were loops with tissue paper hanging down from the end of the loops. On the front was another loop with a bell attached.

"See, honey—hit the paper, hit the paper, ring the bell twice."

97. Ailments of Old Age

Three residents in a retirement facility were comparing their physical problems.

One said, "I've had two knee surgeries, and my diabetes sometimes causes me to pass out."

The second explained, "Without my hearing aids, I can't hear anything quieter than a jet engine, and I have occasional bouts of dementia."

The third responded, "My arthritis is so bad, I can't look right or left, and I can hardly feel my hands or feet."

The third continued, "Isn't it wonderful we still have our driver's licenses!"

98. Dumb Blonde Joke #63

On a layover, the Captain was explaining to a new blonde stewardess where the best places were to eat, shop, and sleep while in this town.

The next morning, while he was briefing his crew, he noticed the new stewardess had not shown up. Knowing the hotel where she stayed, he called her room and asked why she wasn't at the airport.

"I can't get out of my room," she cried.

"Why not?" the Captain asked.

"There are only three doors in my room: one is the bathroom, one is the closet, and the third has a sign on it that says 'Do Not Disturb.'"

99. The Retiring Mailman

When they found out their trusty mailman was going to retire after years of dependable service in all sorts of weather, the residents on a cul-de-sac decided each family would give him a gift. When he arrived at the first house, the family gave him a check for fifty dollars.

At the second home, they presented him with a beautiful suitcase.

A tackle box, with several excellent lures, awaited him at the third home.

The family at the fourth house gave him a leather-bound, traveling game box.

At the last house, he was met by a beautiful woman in a revealing negligee. She took him by the hand and led him up the stairs to a bedroom, where they made passionate love. When he'd had enough, she took him downstairs and prepared a huge breakfast of pancakes, eggs, bacon, and orange juice. When he was completely satisfied, she poured him a steaming cup of coffee. He noticed a dollar bill protruding from under the cup.

"Everything you've given me has been absolutely wonderful and I will never forget you. However, what is the dollar bill for?"

"Well," she replied, "last night when I told my husband this was your last day and the other people all agreed we should recognize your service, I asked him what we should give you.

"He said, 'Screw him. Give him a dollar.'"

"Breakfast was my idea."

100. You Can't Save Seats

An usher was counting vacant seats in the movie theater when he found a man lying across six seats. "Sir, I'm sorry, but you cannot save those seats. Pick the one you want, and the rest of your party will have to find their own seats."

The man did not move, or utter a sound.

The usher repeated his admonition, and still received no response. He called the manager on his cell phone, and explained the situation.

The manager told the man lying on the seats, "Sir, I insist you move, or I'll call the police." Again, there was no response, so the manager called a policeman and explained the problem.

The cop said, "Buddy, get up or I'll have to arrest you." Seeing no response, he said to the manager, "Maybe he's a foreigner and can't understand English."

The manager asked the man, "Where are you from?"

With a pained voice the man replied, "The balcony."

101. When a Woman Lies, She Has a Good Reason

A poor seamstress was walking along a river, when she stumbled and lost her leather thimble in the water. "Oh, God, what am I to do? I can't sew without my thimble."

The Lord dipped his arm into the water, and pulled out a solid-gold thimble. "Is this yours?" he asked.

"No, Lord, it is not."

God put his arm in the water again, and pulled out a diamond-encrusted thimble. "Is this the one?"

"No, Lord."

God put his arm in the water again, and pulled out her leather thimble. "Is this your thimble?"

"Yes, Lord, it is."

"For being so honest," God said, "you may keep all three."

*   *   *

Several years later, the dressmaker and her husband were walking along the river, when he stumbled and fell in the water. "Oh, God, I cannot do without my husband."

God appeared, and put his arm in the water, and pulled out Richard Gere. "Is this your husband?"

"Yes, Lord, it is."

"Liar," roared God.

"Lord, you misinterpret my answer. If I'd said 'No,' you'd have pulled out someone like Brad Pitt. If I said 'No' again, you'd pull out my husband, and there's no way I can take care of three men."

102. The Neighbor's Wash

A couple moved into a new neighborhood and was having their first breakfast in their new home. The woman looked out the window and saw her neighbor hanging wash on an outdoor wash line. "My goodness, those clothes do not look clean. I wonder if the woman knows she needs a new laundry detergent."

Her husband said nothing.

Every time her neighbor hung out her wash to dry, the wife would always make the same remark.

One day she looked out the window and saw the wash was sparkling clean. "My goodness, look how bright those clothes are! I wonder who told her how to wash?"

Her husband said, "I got up early and washed all our windows."

103. The Don's Bookkeeper

A Mafia Don hired a deaf-and-dumb bookkeeper because he believed the man could not testify about what was said at meetings. The man proved very competent, and it took ten years for the mob to uncover the fact he had skimmed 10 million dollars from their accounts.

The Don was furious, and brought his attorney, who was fluent in sign language, to the bookkeeper's office. "Ask him where he hid the 10 million dollars," he ordered the attorney.

The attorney signed the question to the bookkeeper, who signed back, "I don't know what you're talking about."

"What did he say?" asked the Boss.

"He said he doesn't know what you're talking about."

The Mafia Boss pulled out a gun and pressed the muzzle against the bookkeeper's temple. "Tell him if he doesn't tell me right now, I'm going to blow his brains out."

The attorney signed the Boss's ultimatum.

The bookkeeper excitedly signed, "It's hidden at my cousin Vinnie's home, in the backyard, under the kid's sandbox."

The Don asked, "What did he say?"

The attorney replied, "He said you don't have the balls to do it."

104. Energizer Bunny Dies

The world was stunned by the unexpected death of the Energizer Bunny. He was ten years old.

The coroner estimated the time of death at 9:00 PM last night.

Best known as the pink bunny that kept going and going, he was alone in his apartment at the time of his death.

The autopsy revealed he died of acute coronary arrest induced by sexual over-stimulation. Apparently he had put his batteries in backward and kept coming and coming.

105. Distraught New Bride

A girl from a very rich family got married and had just returned from her honeymoon when her mother called. "How was the honeymoon, darling?"

"Oh, Mother, it was just too perfect. Barbados was fantastic, the hotel was fabulous, John was such a gentleman; we had a wonderful time."

"Well, dear, I am pleased it was so satisfactory. It is important to begin a marriage on a happy note."

The girl began to cry.

"Honey, what's wrong?"

"Oh, Mom, John turned into a beast just as soon as we got home! He began to use terrible four-letter words."

"What words did he say?"

"Mom, they were so bad I can't repeat them."

"Come, dear. Your mother knows how vile some men talk. Tell me what he said."

"He began using words like cook, wash, iron, dust . . ."

"You poor dear, gather up your things. You're coming home until John comes to his senses."

106. Anniversary Present

Two ranchers in Montana were talking. "Joe, don't you have a wedding anniversary comin' up?"

"Sure do, Tom."

"Whatcha gonna do this time?"

"Well, for our twentieth, I took Imogene to Alaska.

"For our thirtieth, I thought I'd bring her back."

107. Dumb Blonde Joke #58

A blonde had received her two-week termination notice. When she got home, she prayed, "God, please help me win the lottery. I've lost my job and will not be able to make the payments on my car."

Two weeks went by, and the girl did not win the lottery. "Dear God, please help me win the lottery. They repossessed my car, and if I can't come up with my monthly house payment the bank will foreclose on my house."

Two weeks went by, and she did not win the lottery. "God," she prayed, "why have you forsaken me? I've lost my car and my house. Why won't you let me win the lottery?"

A deep voice answered, "Honey, work with me on this. BUY A TICKET!"

108. Department Store for Husbands

A new department store opened in town where a woman could pick out a husband. The management posted a few rules: when you get off on a floor, you must pick a man from that floor; if you do not pick one of the men, you will return to the first floor and may not return; if you fail to pick any floor, you will return to the first floor and may not enter the store again.

A woman entered the elevator and went to the first floor. A sign on the door stated: "The men on this floor have excellent jobs."

She contemplated the sign and decided his just having a good job was not sufficient reason for picking a husband, so she pressed the button to take her to the next level. The sign read: "The men on this floor have excellent jobs, and love children." This was better she thought, but wondered what types of men were on the floors above.

She advanced to the next floor and the sign read: "The men on this floor have excellent jobs, love children, and enjoy working around the house." *Now we're getting somewhere. The next floor probably has an even better selection of men.*

She pressed the button and went up one more story. The sign read: "The men on this floor have excellent jobs, love children, enjoy working around the house, and are handsome."

The men keep getting better on each floor; I think I'll go up to the next level. The sign on this floor read: "The men on this floor have excellent jobs, love children, enjoy working around the house, are handsome, and are excellent lovers."

Wow, now we're getting somewhere. What can they possibly have to beat that? I'll go up another floor.

The sign read: "There is no next floor. Thank you for proving you can never satisfy a woman. Have a good day!"

109. The Uncooperative Drunk

A cop pulled over a car that was being driven erratically. "Sir, would you please get out of your car."

The driver complied, and the officer said, "I'm going to give you a Breathalyzer test."

"I can't do that," replied the driver.

"Why not?" asked the cop.

"I have asthma, and blowing into the device might trigger an asthma attack. I could die."

"Then I'll have to take a urine sample for a urinalysis, to determine the alcohol level in your blood stream."

"I can't do that."

"Why not?" replied the cop.

"I have diabetes and that could change the electrolyte level and I could have a seizure."

"OK then, I'll need to draw some blood."

"I can't do that."

"Why not?" the officer asked.

"I'm a hemophiliac. I could bleed to death."

"I guess I'll have to go to the old-fashioned way. I want you to walk this line, heel-to-toe."

"I can't do that."

"Why not?" the cop asked dicustedly.

"I'm drunk."

110. The Cooperative Drunk

There was a bar a few miles out of town which had a reputation for serving patrons more alcohol than they should have.

A cop was trying to get evidence to shut the place down, so at closing time he concealed his squad car in the shadows. Sure enough, a man stumbled out the door and beat an unsteady path to a car. He fumbled with his keys and dropped them. Cautiously, he bent down to pick them up and fell against the car. When he finally retrieved his keys and tried to insert one in the door, it didn't fit, so he wove his way to the next car. The key didn't fit that car either.

By this time, most of the other patrons had left, but the cop was determined to arrest this man.

Soon, the man came to the last car in the parking lot, inserted his key, opened the door, and entered the car. He switched on the engine and tromped on the accelerator. The officer started his engine and drove behind the drunk's car, with all his lights flashing. "Get out of the car," the officer ordered.

The man complied.

"I'm going to administer a Breathalyzer test to you."

The man readily agreed.

The test proved the man to be cold sober.

"I don't understand this. A minute ago you looked like you were about to pass out."

The man laughed. "Tonight I was the designated decoy."

111. Ode to a Married Man

From 20 to 30, if a man lives right, it's once in the morning and once at night.

From 30 to 40, if a man lives right, it's once in the morning or once at night.

From 40 to 50, it's now and then.

From 50 to 60, it's God knows when.

From 60 to 70, if he's still inclined, don't let him fool you; it's all in his mind.

112. Old Prospector

An old prospector and his tired old mule walk into a western town. He's been out in the hills for about six months without a drop of whisky. Stopping at the first saloon, he ties his mule to the hitching rail. As he stands there, brushing the dust from his clothes, a young man walks out of the saloon with a gun in one hand and a bottle of whisky in the other.

The young gunslinger looks at the old man and laughs, saying, "Hey, old man, do you like to dance?"

The prospector smiles and replies, "Nope, I never danced. I just never wanted to."

A crowd collected as the gunslinger said, "Well, you old coot, you're gonna dance now," and starts shooting at the old man's feet.

The prospector begins hopping up and down, and everyone is laughing at his plight.

When the man has fired his last round, he holsters his gun and turns to enter the saloon.

The old man reaches up on his mule, pulls out his double-barreled shotgun, and pulls back both hammers, making a double-clicking sound.

The gunslinger hears the double click and everything gets very quiet. The crowd, who had been laughing moments before, watches as the gunfighter turns slowly around, looking down both barrels of the shotgun.

The old prospector asks, "Sonny, did you ever kiss a mule's ass?"

The young man, chokes, swallows hard, and says, "No, but I've always wanted to."

The moral: don't waste ammunition, and don't mess with old people. There are reasons why they managed to get old.

113. Grandmother Needs Contraceptive Pills

An elderly woman consulted her doctor about a prescription for contraceptive pills.

"Margaret," the doctor advised, "you're well past child-bearing age. You don't need to worry about getting pregnant."

"I don't use them to keep from getting pregnant. I use them to sleep better."

"Sleeping pills?" the doctor inquired. Contraceptive pills don't help you to sleep."

"Oh yes they do! My granddaughter just came to live with me, and I slip one of them into her orange juice every morning. Believe me, I sleep a lot better."

114. Sailor Meets Punk Rocker

A sailor is sitting in a car in the London Underground when a punk rocker comes in and sits across from him. The young man has a Mohawk hair-style, colored red, green, yellow, and blue.

The sailor keeps starring at the man.

The punk rocker asks, "What's the matter, old man? Haven't you seen different-colored hair before?"

"Yes," the sailor replies. "I was just thinking. I was drunk in Java once and made love to a parrot; I thought you might be my son."

115. Differences between Black Bears and Brown Bears

The Fish & Wildlife Service has issued a caution to hikers to beware of bears. The Service recommends sewing small silver bells to your clothing to alert bears of your presence, so they can avoid you. They recommend hikers carry pepper spray in case of attack if you inadvertently come upon a bear.

The Service also recommends you scan bear feces to determine whether you are in a black bear or brown bear habitat. Black bear feces, or scat, usually consist of berry seeds, feathers, and mouse hair. Brown bear scat has a pungent pepper smell and contains small silver bells.

116. Praying Parrots

A woman purchased a female parrot which was raised in a house of prostitution. Every time she saw a man, the parrot would say, "Hi, how about a little loving?"

The woman consulted her priest about the problem.

The priest told her, "I have three parrots that say the rosary and pray all day. I think they would be a good influence on your parrot."

When the woman brought her parrot to the priest's residence, they placed her in the cage with the other birds, and she said, "Hi, boys, want to party?"

One of the priest's parrots said, "Drop the beads, fellas—our prayers are answered."

117. Tough Old Cowboy

An old cowboy told his son, "If you want to live to an old age and be healthy all the time, have pinch of gun-powder with every meal."

The young man followed his father's advice and lived to be 93, was never sick a day in his life, and left a 16-foot crater where the crematorium used to be.

118. Three Sparrows

A parade went by on Michigan Avenue, and three sparrows hopped down and began eating horse apples on the street. When they'd eaten their fill, they flew to the handle of an old-fashioned water pump. They sat for a short while and one sparrow said, "I guess I'd better get home, it's getting dark."

The little bird took off, and, after flying ten feet, died in mid-air.

That event shook up the other two sparrows, who decided they'd eaten too much and elected to let the food digest a bit.

Finally, the second sparrow said, "The wife will kill me if I don't get home quickly," so he took off, flew a hundred feet, and dropped dead.

The third sparrow sat there until the moon rose; he then decided he'd waited long enough and flew two hundred feet before he, too, dropped dead.

The moral of this story is—don't fly off the handle when you're full of shit.

119. Hard of Hearing

On a road trip, a man and his wife pulled into a gas station. The attendant asked the man, "Do you want me to fill it up?"

The driver told him to go ahead.

The wife asked, "What did he say?"

"He asked if he should fill the gas tank."

While the pump was running, the attendant asked, "Do you want me to check the oil?"

The driver nodded in the affirmative.

The wife asked, "What did he say?"

Her husband replied, "He asked if he should check the oil."

After the tank was filled, and the driver had paid the bill, the attendant asked, "Where are you headed?"

"Rochester, New York," replied the driver.

"Rochester," the attendant answered. "That's the town where I had the worst lay in my life."

"What did he say?" asked the wife.

"He said he thinks he knows you,"

120. Sex in Florida

An elderly couple went to a sex therapist, and asked him to watch how they made love so he could tell them how they could improve.

The therapist observed the couple's copulation, told them they were performing perfectly, and collected his fee of $75.

A week later, they appeared again, and asked him to see if they could improve their sexual activity.

Again, the therapist observed them, and said there was nothing he could recommend to improve their sexual skills, and collected his $75 fee.

A week later, the couple appeared at the therapist's office again.

"Why do you keep coming back? I've told you, you're doing it perfectly."

"Well," said the man, "she's married. I'm married. The Hyatt charges $150. The Holiday Inn charges $85. You charge $75, and Medicare gives me a $58 refund."

121. The Condom

Miss Tully, a 70-year-old spinster, had been the church's organist for nearly 50 years. The new minister was visiting his parishioners and had called upon Miss Tully.

"Good afternoon, Parson. Please come in. Would you like some coffee or tea?" she asked.

"Coffee would be fine, Miss Tully. I've come to ask you if you'd continue to be our organist."

"Of course, Parson, I'd be honored to play for our congregation. Please excuse me while I fix the coffee."

The Parson looked about the sitting room and saw a beautiful, old pump organ. The organ was to be expected, but what caught his attention was a small crystal bowl, with a condom floating in water, sitting on a lace doily atop the organ. For the life of him, he couldn't comprehend why a 70-year-old spinster would have a condom floating in a glass bowl.

When Miss Tully returned, and they were sipping their coffee, the Parson was compelled to ask, "Miss Tully, what is that on top of your organ?"

"It's just wonderful. I found it on the street one day. It was in a foil wrapper that said 'To prevent disease, keep moist and place on organ.' Would you believe I haven't had a cold all winter?"

122. Change Vacation Procedure

Two not-too-bright boys were talking. "Billy Joe, what are you going to do on your vacation?" asked one.

"I think I'm a-gonna to do somethin' different this time."

"What you gonna do different?"

"Well, I went to Hawaii, and Ermaline got pregnant. Then I went to the Bahamas, and Ermaline got pregnant. I went to Tahiti, and Ermaline got pregnant. This time I'm goin' to take her with me."

123. City Boys Go Duck Hunting

Two New York businessmen decide to try their luck at duck hunting. That fall, they head to the lakes of Vermont, and stop at a small store advertising hunting licenses and equipment. They buy their duck hunting licenses, and rent a row boat.

The proprietor says, "Boys, I can see you're not experienced duck hunters, so, if you'd like, I'll loan you my golden retriever. He's won several awards for getting ducks."

"That would be a help," declares one of the New Yorkers.

"You just pick him up tomorrow about 5 AM, when you head out to the lake. You'll find a duck blind in the reeds right near shore, at the end of the road."

The men pick up the dog and boat, and trudge to the lake. They climb into the boat and hide in the duck blind. After three hours, the two guys are freezing and haven't gotten a single duck.

"I'm tired of this," one man complained. "This duck hunting is for the birds. We can't seem to get a single duck."

"I keep telling you," the other replied. "We aren't throwing the dog high enough."

124. Mississippi Boys Go Ice Fishing

Two boys from Mississippi decide to try their hand at ice fishing. They head up to Minnesota and stop at a store on Little Sand Lake.

"Y'all sell fishin' licenses?" Luke asks the store owner.

"Sure, boys, is this your first time ice fishing?"

"Yes, sir, it shore is," replied Billy Bob.

As they were leaving the store, the proprietor asked, "Did you bring an ice pick to cut through the ice?"

"No, sir, we shore didn't. Ya got some fer sale?"

"Sure, fellas, just a buck apiece."

The Mississippi boys bought two, and set off to the lake.

About an hour later, Billy Bob came back and asked, "Does ya have any more ice picks?"

The store keeper sold him two more.

Another hour later, Luke came up and asked, "How many more of them ice picks ya got?'

The storekeeper said, "I've got just six more."

"I'll take 'em all." replied Luke.

"Tell me, son. Why do you need more ice picks?"

" 'Cause we ain't even got the boat in the water yet"

125. The Brothel Parrot

(An 80+ year-old joke)

A woman visited a pet shop and spotted a large beautifully-colored parrot. There was a sign on the cage that said $50.

"Why so cheap?" she asked the shop owner.

"I must tell you; this parrot came from a brothel the cops just closed up. Sometimes it says some pretty vulgar words."

The woman thought for a while, and decided she'd take the bird anyway.

She placed the cage in the living room, took the cover off, and waited for the parrot to say something.

It looked around and said, "Ooooo, new house. Ooooo, new madam."

The woman thought of the implications of the bird's words, but thought the idea was kind of cute.

Later, her two daughters came home and the parrot said, "Ooooo, new house. Ooooo, new madam. Ooooo, new girls."

The girls and their mother were a bit offended, but then began to laugh about the situation. "Boy," said one of the girls, "daddy will have a fit when he comes home.

"I can't wait to see the expression on his face when he hears what the parrot says," replied her sister.

A few minutes later, their father came home.

The parrot looked at him and said, "Hi, Keith."

126. O'Brian Leaves a Trail

Sean O'Brian stumbled home from O'Leary's Bar. He fumbled his keys, but finally gets the front door open. As he takes the first step up the stairs he loses his balance, and lands flat on his butt, breaking the pint whiskey bottle he has in his back pocket. Too intoxicated to care, he makes it to the bathroom and removes his clothes. Peering over his shoulder at the mirror on the door, he tries to see what is burning his ass. When his vision clears, he perceives several cuts where the bottle had broken; rivulets of blood flow down from each cut. O'Brian opens the medicine cabinet and takes out the box of Band-Aids, and proceeds to meticulously cover each wound. Satisfied with his work, he goes to bed.

Early the next morning, Kate, his wife, barges into the bedroom and says, "Mr. O'Brian, you really tied one on last night, didn't you?"

"Katy, me darlin', whatever gave ye that idea?"

"Me first clue was the front door was open all night. The second clue was the broken glass and smell of whiskey at the bottom of the stairs. The last clue was all the Band-Aids stuck to the bathroom mirror."

127. Coincidences

A man was seated at Mallory's bar, sipping a beer, when a gentleman comes up to him and says, "I can tell by your accent that you come from the old sod."

"Aye, that I do, sir."

"What a coincidence! So do I, that calls for a drink," the gentleman suggests.

After a short while, the first fellow inquires, "Where in Ireland do ye come from?"

"County Killarney," replies the gentleman.

"Well, by God, I come from there meself. What a coincidence! That calls for another drink."

After they'd finished their beers, the gentleman asks, "What high school did ye attend?"

"Why, St. Catherine's, of course."

"Jesus, Joseph, and Mary, I went there me self!" exclaims the gentleman.

Just then a new customer enters in and asks Mallory, "How's things going tonight, Mallory?"

"Same as usual," he answers, "except the Clancy twins are drunk again."

128. Mother Superior and the Construction Foreman

Construction had started on the vacant lot next to a convent, and the Mother Superior was becoming more and more upset with the vile language used by the construction workers in the course of their operations.

Finally, she had had enough, and she strode into the construction yard and yelled, "Who's in charge here?"

A burly man came out of the construction office trailer office and replied, "I am, Sister. What can I do for you?"

"I'm in charge of the convent next door. I am responsible for twenty novices undergoing instruction. The foul language your men use is very upsetting to them. I strongly request you to tell your men to be more careful in their choice of words."

"Mother, you have to understand, construction people call a spade, a spade."

"That would be eminently satisfactory. Just tell them to quit referring to it as a fucking shovel!"

129. Little Girl Hired by Construction Crew

A little six-year-old girl was fascinated by the new home being constructed in the adjacent lot. One day she strolled over and talked to the workmen, who took a liking to her. They asked if she would like to help them.

The little girl readily agreed, and they gave her small jobs to do, such as bringing nails, a hammer, a sandwich, or other simple tasks. At the end of the week the men got together and gave her a "paycheck" in an envelope.

The girl took it home and explained how the men paid her for helping them.

Her mother advised her to open a savings account at the local bank, so her money would be safe.

At the bank, the little girl said, "I'd like to open a savings account and deposit my money."

The clerk asked, "How did you get the money?"

"I earned it helping the construction crew next door."

"Do you think you'll work next week?" asked the woman.

"I will if the bastards from Home Depot deliver the fucking drywall."

130. Irish Lottery

(Updated from the Irish Sweepstakes)

Sam, a Jewish tailor, won $2,000,000 in the Irish National Lottery. He had just learned of his good luck, when the Internal Revenue Service notified him he would owe the government $800,000.

Sam went to his friend Sol, an attorney, and complained, "Sol, I'm a poor Jewish tailor, and I won two million dollars in the Irish Lottery. Uncle Sam says I owe him eight hundred thousand. How can I keep all of it and retire?"

Sol, replied, "It's simple, Sam. All you have to do is emigrate to Ireland and become an Irish citizen. Then you can keep it all, and it'll be tax-free."

So Sam applied for Irish citizenship and flew to Shannon airport in Dublin.

He walked up to the custom's agent and said, "I'm Sam the tailor, and I've come to become an Irish citizen."

After checking his passport and visa, the agent directed Sam to the medical office.

Sam walked in and announced, "I'm Sam the tailor, and I've come to become an Irish citizen."

The receptionist had Sam fill out several forms, and when he had finished, she handed the papers to him and instructed, "Go through that door, and hand the papers to the doctor."

Sam did as he was told and entered the doctor's office, announcing, "I'm Sam the tailor, and I've come to be an Irish citizen."

The old Irish doctor looked up and said, "Tyke of yer clothes and put em on the table."

Sam did as instructed and began to disrobe. When he dropped his drawers, the doctor exclaimed, "Faith, ya can't become an Irish citizen!"

Sam replied, "Vy not?"

"Ye been circumcised."

"What's the matter? Ya gotta be a complete prick to be an Irishman?"

131. Swedish Volunteer in the RAF

During the early stages of WWII, the British were seeking volunteers to fly in the RAF. As part of their campaign, they brought pilots from other countries to speak to American audiences in hopes of enticing young men to join conflict in Britain. One such speaker was Flight Lieutenant Johansson, a Swedish volunteer, who was to address a ladies' garden club.

"Ladies," said the hostess, "it is my pleasure to introduce Flight Lieutenant Johansson, a Swedish officer in the RAF. He will explain the need for American fighter pilots at this crucial time in the Battle of Britain."

"Tank you, ladies. I tink I'll tell you how I became an Ace in one day. Dare I vas sippin oxygen at twenty-tousan feet ven I zee tree Yerman fuckers at ten tousan feet. I did an Immelman und ving over, und come down an shot the rear fucker, then swung over and shot the lead fucker . . ."

"Excuse me, Flight Lieutenant. Ladies, Lieutenant Johansson has an accent, and is referring to the German Fokker aircraft."

"No, lady, dem fuckers were flyin' Messerschmitts."

132. The Hard Way

A man was driving the back roads of Tennessee when he came upon a strange sight: a man pulling a plow while his mule guided the plow. He couldn't resist stopping and finding what the story was.

He stopped the car and went up to the fence. "Sir, would you please tell me why you are pulling the plow instead of the mule?"

"Why sure, son, I like to do things the hard way!"

"Thank you. It was so unusual I had to ask. I wonder if I could drive up to your house and get a drink of water?"

"Sure, I'll be up in about ten minutes."

"I can drive you up."

"Nope. As I said, I like to do things the hard way. I'll just walk across the field."

The man drove to the house and waited.

Finally, the farmer got to the house and said, "Step around back to the well."

The well had a rope fixed to a wooden axle with a crank arm. A bucket was tied to the end of the rope. The farmer lowered the bucket to the water, picked up a tin cup, stepped over the edge, and began to climb down the rope.

The man observed, "I understand why you don't use the bucket to bring the water up; you like to do things the hard way."

"You're right. I'll be up in a couple of minutes." Slowly the man climbed up the rope with one arm while he held on to the cup filled with water. "Here you are, son—nice and cold."

Just then the farmer's wife appeared. She was in a full body cast, with a broken arm held in front of her as she hobbled out on a crutch.

"My God, was she in an auto accident?"

"Nope, we were making love standing up in a hammock."

133. The Ventriloquist

A ventriloquist was traveling from a gig in Chicago to one in Nevada. After he passed through Albuquerque he came upon an Indian, riding a horse, who was driving a flock of sheep across the road. The Indian's dog raced around the flock to keep them moving.

The ventriloquist pulled off, and waited until the sheep cleared the road. He thought he'd have a little fun with the Indian, and as the horse passed he asked, "Horse, how does the Indian treat you?"

He threw his voice to sound as if the horse were speaking. "He makes me carry him all day. The only time I get to rest is at night, and he doesn't give me enough food, so I have to munch on dry desert grass."

The Indian stopped his horse. The dog stood at the feet of the horse.

The ventriloquist said, "Dog, how does your master treat you?"

The dog appeared to reply, "He makes me run around the sheep all day. He doesn't give me enough food or water, and he makes me sleep in the cold every night."

The ventriloquist looked at an ewe and asked, "How does the Indian treat you?"

The Indian finally spoke: "Sheep, her lie."

134. The Sculpture of the Four Goddesses

A redneck from Arkansas visited the National Museum of Art and asked one of the guards, "Can ya tell me whar that statue of the four goddesses is?"

The guard replied, "Yes, sir. Straight down the main corridor, second hallway to your left. I'll be down in a few minutes to explain what the artist had in mind when he sculpted it."

"Thank ya," said the redneck, as he walked toward the main corridor.

When he located the sculpture, he studied it for a while. It had four naked women equally spaced in a circular fashion facing the center. The first had a surprised look upon her face; her eyes and mouth were wide open and her arms were down at her sides palms outward. The statue to her right was pointing to the figure directly across, which was standing in a boxing pose. The last figure, which was directly across from the first, had her hands covering her face.

The guard appeared and remarked, "I see you've found our famous sculpture. Would you like me to explain what the artist was trying to portray?"

"I think I got it figgered out, but go ahead."

The guard said, "The first woman is the Goddess of Surprise. The second is the Goddess of Direction. The third portrays the Goddess of Self-defense. The last is the Goddess of Shame. Is that what you thought?"

"Purdy close," the man replied. "Ah figgered the first said 'Who farted?' The second said, 'She did.' The third said, 'I did not.' And the last one said, 'I did.'"

135. The Diesel Fitter

Two men were standing in the unemployment compensation line. The women's intimate clothing factory, where they had worked, had closed down.

The second man overheard the compensation specialist tell his friend he was to receive $200 per month.

When his turn came, the woman asked what job he performed at the factory. He replied, "I was a crotch stitcher on the women's panty hose line."

"Well," she replied, "I believe your compensation will be $150 a month."

"Wait a minute," the man replied. "You gave my buddy $200 a month, why the difference?"

"He had a highly skilled job as a diesel fitter. So he receives additional compensation."

"He worked right next to me on the line. I'd hand the finished panty hose to him. He'd jam them down over his head and say, 'Dees'l fit her.'"

136. Cold Water Clean

A young man drove into the hills to visit his grandfather. The nearest town was 60 miles away. As he pulled into the yard, a dog came to greet him. Patting the dog's head, he said, "Good dog," and walked up to the house.

They had dinner that evening. The grandson noticed some food particles on the dishes and utensils. "Grandpa, these dishes don't look too clean."

"Grandson, we cain't have all them niceties you have in town. The dishes are as clean as cold water can get them."

The next morning, at breakfast, the young man again noticed the dishes were not very clean, but kept it to himself.

At lunch time the young man was bored and said to his grandfather, "Grandpa, after lunch, I think I'll go into town, if it's OK with you."

"That'll be fine, son; we'll have dinner right soon."

Looking at the plates, the young man noticed egg yolk on his plate and fork. "Grandpa, these plates are not clean."

"Like I done told you, they're as clean as cold water can get em."

After their meal, the grandson walked to his car and the dog snarled at him as he opened the gate. "Grandpa, the dog won't let me pass."

"Dammit, Cold Water, let him be."

137. Dumb Blonde Joke #123

A cop pulls over a blonde driver doing 80 mph in a 50 mph zone. "Ma'am, may I see your driver's license, please?"

"Will you people please make up your mind? You took it away from me yesterday."

138. Intelligent Rooster

A man from a local agriculture department gave a presentation to farmers in his region on how they might become more productive while also giving them more time to rest.

One of the hints he came up with was to hang a bell around each rooster's neck. Each bell was to have a different sound so the farmer could distinguish which rooster was performing his reproductive duties. In that way the farmer could cull the most inefficient roosters from his flock.

Farmer Jones decided to give the technique a try, so he had bells with different tones placed on each rooster's neck, and sat back in his rocking chair with a tally book in his lap, recording how often each bird did his thing. All went well, until he realized his oldest rooster had quit performing, so he went to the chicken coop and watched what was going on. While the three other males would jump onto a pullet, which would elicit a screech, the oldest took the bell in its beak, crept up on a hen, did his job, and jumped off before the hen had a chance to protest. He thought this was a very intelligent rooster, so he took the bird to the State Fair.

The judges observed the rooster's performance and awarded it two prizes: the No—Bell Prize and the Pullet Surprise.

139. Woman Rancher and Her Gay Foreman

After her husband died, the widow found she needed help in running the ranch so she advertised for a foreman. Two men applied; one was capable, but had a history of drunkenness; the second was also capable, but was an admitted homosexual.

She thought the drunk might get loaded and rape her, so she hired the gay man.

He proved eminently satisfactory, and after three months she told him they both deserved a weekend off.

They both went to town; the woman came back late Saturday night. On Sunday she was waiting in the bunk house when he arrived. She said, "Ted, take off my blouse."

He complied.

She then said, "Now take off my skirt."

Again he did as ordered.

"Now, take off my bra."

He complied.

Finally, she demanded, "Take off my panties."

He did.

"Now," she snapped, "if you ever wear my clothes again, you're fired."

140. Irish Castaway

An Irishman had been a castaway on a deserted island for 10 years, 2 months and 3 days when he observed a speck on the ocean. As he watched, he saw it was a woman in a wetsuit swimming toward shore.

When she walked out of the water, she asked, "How long have you been on this island?"

He replied, "10 years, 2 months and 3 days."

She zipped open a pouch and pulled out a packet of three cigars. "How long has it been since you had a good Cuban cigar?"

"10 years, 2 months and 3 days."

She cut off the end of a cigar, handed it to him, and then lit it from a lighter from another pocket in the arm of the wetsuit.

He puffed on the cigar and said, "Begorra, tis delightful. Thank you."

The woman unzipped another pocket and asked, "How long since you've had a snort of good Irish whiskey?"

"10 years, 2 months and 3 days."

She handed him the flask, and he took a big swig. "Lord love us, I thought I'd die before I tasted the nectar of the Gods again."

The woman began unzipping the main zipper of her suit and asked, "How long has it been since you played around?"

"Jesus, Joseph, and Mary, don't tell me ya got a set of clubs in that suit of yours?"

141. Searching for Their Wives in Wal-Mart

Two old men bumped into one another in a giant Wal-Mart. "I'm sorry," said one. "I was looking for my wife and didn't see you."

"That's OK," replied the second. "I was looking for my wife, too. What does yours look like?"

"She's beautiful, about five-foot-five, weighs 125 pounds, has red hair, is 23-years old, wearing short-short red pants, and a tight white blouse. What's yours look like?"

The second man replied, "Let's look for yours first."

142. The Cowboy and the Lesbian

A cowboy, in full regalia—Stetson, Levi's, chaps, red bandana, plaid shirt, boots—

is sitting at a table in a bar when a woman sits down at his table and looks at him. She asks, "Are you a real cowboy?"

"Yes, ma'am, I guess I am. I've been punching cattle, riding fence-lines, branding cattle and breaking horses all my life. What are you?"

"I'm a lesbian."

"What's a lesbian?" he inquires.

"I think about women all the time, when I'm eating, taking a shower, even when I'm sleeping."

"I see," said the cowboy.

After the woman leaves, the cowboy orders another beer and is sitting back and enjoying it when a man comes in and asks, "Are you a real cowboy?"

"I thought I was. But I just found out I'm a lesbian."

143. Dumb Blonde Joke #245

A blonde's BMW is towed into a garage. She asks the mechanic if he can tell her what is wrong with it.

"Just as soon as I can inspect it, I'll tell you," he replies.

A short while later he drives it to the front. "Here it is, just as good as new, ma'am."

"What was wrong with it?" the blonde asks.

"Just crap in the carburetor."

"How often should I do that?" she inquires.

144. Old Rooster vs. Young Rooster

An old rooster awoke one morning to find a young rooster strutting around the yard.

"Good morning, you old coot," says the youngster. "Can't you see you're not needed around here anymore? You better get back to your roost and stay there. I'm king of this flock now."

The old rooster replies, "I may be a little slower now, but I can still do my job. I'll tell you how to settle this problem."

"How's that?" asks the young upstart.

"We'll race around the barn twice. If you win, I leave. If I win, you leave. Because I'm old, you give me a handicap of five yards."

"I could spot you ten yards and still beat you."

"OK," said the old rooster as he took his position. "Ready? Set. Go!"

The two birds were screeching and squawking as they went around the barn the first time. As they made the final round, the young rooster said, "Goodbye, you old coot; I'm going to pass you now."

Just then the farmer leveled his shotgun and shot the young rooster. "Damn," he observed, "that's the third queer rooster I've bought in the past two months."

145. Doctor's Slight Error

A woman returned home from visiting her doctor and reviewed the prescription he had given her. She immediately called the office and asked to speak to the physician.

When he came on the line and asked what her problem was, she asked, "Didn't you say I was going to have to take this medicine the rest of my life?"

"Yes, I did tell you that. Why do you ask?"

"Is there something you didn't tell me about my health?"

"No. I told you everything."

"Then why does the prescription say 'No refills'?"

146. Getting into Heaven

A young man appeared before St. Peter at the Pearly Gates.

"Tell me, young man, what have you done to warrant entry into Heaven?"

"Well, sir," the man replied, "While driving through the Black Hills of Dakota, I saw a girl being molested by a bunch of Hell's Angels bikers. I stopped my car and went over to their leader, grabbed him by his nose ring, tore it out, smacked him in the jaw, and kicked over his bike.

"Then I told them to leave the girl alone, and if any one objected they could try to take a piece of me."

"Wow!" exclaimed St. Peter, "that was really brave. When did this happen?"

The man looked at his watch and replied, "About three minutes ago."

147. Elderly Hearing Test

After completing their yearly physical, the elderly gentleman asked the doctor, "Doc, I think Edie is becoming hard of hearing, and refuses to take a hearing test. Is there anything I can do to convince her she needs hearing-aids?"

"Well," replied the doctor, "there's a simple test you can try at home. Stand about twenty feet behind her and ask a question in a normal voice. If she doesn't hear you, move about ten feet away and ask the same question again. If you get no response, move directly behind her and ask again."

That night as his wife was fixing dinner, her husband asked, "Dear, what's for dinner?" Not getting a response, he moved ten feet behind her and asked again. She gave no reply, so he moved directly behind her and asked what she was preparing for dinner.

"For the third time, Henry, it's ham casserole."

148. What Kind of Animal Are You?

One morning a blind bunny was hopping down the bunny trail and tripped over a large snake and fell, kerplop, right on his little twitchy nose.

"Oh, please excuse me," he said. "I didn't mean to trip over you, but I'm blind and can't see."

"That's perfectly all right," replied the snake. "To be sure, it was my fault. I didn't mean to trip you, but I'm blind, too, and I didn't see you coming. By the way, what kind of animal are you?"

"Well, I really don't know," said the bunny. "I'm blind, and I've never seen myself. Maybe you could examine me and find out."

So the snake felt the bunny all over, and said, "Well, you're soft, and cuddly, and you have long silky ears, and a little fluffy tail, and a dear twitchy little nose. You must be a bunny rabbit."

The bunny said, "I can't thank you enough. But, by the way, what kind of animal are you?"

The snake replied that he didn't know either, and the bunny agreed to examine him. When the bunny was finished feeling the snake all over, the snake asked, "Well, what kind of animal am I?"

The bunny replied, "You're cold, you're slippery, and you haven't got any balls. You must be a politician."

149. Bringing a Hairdryer through Customs

A distinguished-appearing young woman, on a flight from Ireland to the U.S., asked the priest sitting beside her, "Father, may I ask a favor?"

"Of course, child, what may I do for you?"

"Well, I bought an expensive woman's electronic hairdryer for my mother's birthday. It is unopened and well over the Custom's limits, and I'm afraid they'll confiscate it. Is there any way you could carry it through customs for me—under your robes, for instance?"

"I would love to help you, my dear, but I must warn you; I will not lie."

"With your honest face, Father, no one will question you."

When they got to Customs, she let the priest go first. The official asked, "Father, do you have anything to declare?"

"From the top of my head to my waist, I have nothing to declare."

Thinking this was a strange response, the agent asked, "And what do you have to declare below your waist?"

"I have a marvelous instrument designed to be used on a woman, but which is, to date, unused."

Roaring with laughter, the customs agent said, "Go ahead, Father."

150. The Church Gossip

Clara, the church gossip, and self-appointed monitor of the congregation's morals, kept sticking her nose into other people's business. Several members did not approve of her extra-curricular activities, but feared her enough to keep their thoughts to themselves.

She made a mistake, however, when she accused Elmer, a new member, of being an alcoholic, after seeing Elmer's old pick-up truck outside of the town's only bar one afternoon. She emphatically told Elmer (and several others) that everyone seeing it there would know exactly what he was doing.

Elmer, a man of few words, stared at Clara for a moment, then just turned and walked away.

Later that evening, Elmer quietly parked his pick-up in front of Clara's house, walked home, and left it there all night.

151. The Pope Orders a Pizza

Gino owned a pizza bakery just outside the Vatican. One day he received a call from the Papacy that the Pope wanted a pepperoni and hamburger pizza. When Gino arrived at St. Peter's Square, he found it packed with people. He went up to one of the Swiss Guards and told him of his plight.

The guard immediately parted the crowd, and Gino delivered his pizza.

Arriving back at the Square, which was still packed with people, Gino requested the guard take him back to the entrance, as he had several pies cooking that would be burned if he did not return quickly.

The guard replied, "I'll take you back if you'll give me half the tip you received from the Pope."

Gino was in no position to argue, and agreed to the guard's demand.

When they arrived at the entrance, the guard said, "OK, give me half of your tip."

Gino faced him, and gave him half of the Sign of the Cross!

152. Wanted: an Authentic- looking Pirate

In response to an ad in *Variety* for an authentic looking pirate, a man walked up to the casting director and asked, "Will I fit the part?"

The casting director was amazed. The man had a patch over one eye, a peg leg, and a hook for his left hand. "You're perfect! Could you tell me how you lost your lower right leg?"

"It was in the Celebes, a few years back. Some pirates attacked me ship, and a lucky shot from a canon cut it off at the knee."

"How about your hook?" the director inquired.

"Aye, that was in the Dry Tortugas about five years ago. Again, some pirates tried to take me ship, and I got it cut off in a sword fight."

"Lord, man," the director exclaimed. "You've really had some dangerous adventures. How did you lose your eye?"

"Well," said the man, "I was looking up at me sails when a gull pooped in me eye."

The director looked at him, and said, "I had no idea that gull poop could put out an eye."

"No," the man replied, "it was the first day I got me hook."

153. Only a Mother Would Know

One day my mother was out, and my dad was in charge of me.

I was maybe 2½ years old. Someone had given me a little tea set as a gift. It was one of my most favorite toys.

Daddy was in the living room, engrossed in the evening news, when I brought daddy a pot of "tea" and a tea cup. The "tea" was just water. After a couple of more cups of tea for daddy, and lots of praise for such yummy tea, my mom came home.

Daddy made her wait in the living room and watch me pour him a cup of tea, because it was "just the cutest thing!"

Mom waited, and watched daddy drink a cup of my tea.

Then she said, as only a mother would know, "Dear, did it ever occur to you that the only place she can reach to get water is the toilet?"

154. Shady Acres Retirement Home

A man took his father to visit several retirement homes. After spending the morning and most of the afternoon in a futile search for a proper home for his father, they came upon Shady Acres, a very sumptuous and complete facility.

Sitting in the office, going over all the amenities and costs, the old man began to slowly tip to one side of his chair.

An attendant immediately rushed over and straightened the man up.

As the conversation went on, the old man began to slowly tip to his right.

Again the attendant straightened him up. When the son had gotten all the particulars, he and his father made their way to the car. As they walked along, the son said, "I think we finally found the right retirement home for you, Dad."

The old man replied, "I don't like Shady Acres!"

"My God, Dad, why not? It's got everything you like—a golf course, putting green, bowling alley, great food, and a beautiful private room."

"Shady Acres won't let you fart."

155. Equally Qualified Job Applicants

Two men applied for an engineering position at a large electronics firm. The personnel manager was surprised their qualifications and experience were so closely matched.

"Gentlemen, I can't differentiate between the two of you, so I've decided to give you a test. The one with the best score gets the job."

After they handed in their tests, the manager was amazed they both missed the fourth question. "Though you both scored the same on the test, I've decided to award the job to Mr. Smith."

"How can you give Smith the job when we both missed the same question?" asked Mr. Jones, the other applicant.

"Mr. Smith's answer was, 'I don't know.'"

"You answered, "me either.'"

156. Dumb Blonde Joke #24

A blonde walked into a department store and said to the clerk, "I'd like to buy this TV."

The clerk responded, "We don't sell to blondes."

Highly upset, the woman dashed out of the store.

The next day she reappeared, and told a different floor clerk that she'd like to buy the TV she had looked at the day before.

Again the salesman said, "I'm sorry. But we don't sell to blondes."

Infuriated, she stormed out of the store, and made her way to a beauty parlor, where she had her hair dyed and restyled.

The next day, confidant the clerks would not recognize her, she strode into the store and told the salesman of the TV she wished to purchase.

Again the clerk replied, "I'm sorry, we don't sell to blondes."

"How can you tell I'm a blonde?" she demanded.

"Because the TV you want is a microwave."

157. Grandfather

A woman in a grocery store happens upon a grandpa and his poorly behaving three-year-old grandson. It is obvious the man has his hands full with the kid screaming for candy in the candy aisle; cookies in the cookie aisle; the same for the fruit, cereal, and soda aisles. Meanwhile, the old man is working his way around, saying in a controlled voice, "Easy, Albert, we won't be long, easy boy."

Another outburst from the child, and she hears his grandfather calmly say, "Keep calm, Albert, just a couple more minutes and we'll be out of here."

At the checkout, the little terror begins throwing things from the cart, and gramps, again in a controlled voice, says, "Albert, Albert, relax buddy, don't get upset, we'll be home in five minutes; stay cool, Al."

Very impressed, the woman goes up to the old man as he's loading the kid and groceries into the car and says, "Sir, it's none of my business, but you were amazing back there. I don't know how you did it. The whole time you kept your composure, no matter how loud and disruptive the boy got. You just calmly kept saying things would be OK. Albert is very lucky to have you as his grandfather."

"Thanks, lady," said the man. "But I'm Albert; the little bastard's name is Johnny."

158. The Magic Frog

A golfer's ball lands a few feet from a pond. The man takes out a club and is addressing the ball, when he hears, "Ribbit, six iron."

He looks around and sees a frog staring at him. "Did you say something?" he asks.

"Yes," replies the frog. "Use a six iron."

"I can make it with a seven," retorts the man.

"Use a six iron," the frog insists.

The golfer exchanges his seven iron for a six, and then strokes the ball, which lands a foot from the cup. He picks up the frog and slips it into his pocket. At the next hole he asks the frog, "Driver or two wood?"

"Two wood," the frog replies.

So it went through the rest of the holes, and the golfer was astounded that he had the best round of golf in his life.

"What should we do next?" the golfer asks the frog.

"Ribbit, Las Vegas," the frog answers.

At the first casino, the golfer is walking past the roulette table when the frog says, "Ribbit, $500 on 35."

As instructed, the man puts the chips on 35. Amazingly, the ball comes to rest on 35.

"What next?" the man inquires.

"Get a suite of rooms," instructs the frog.

In the luxurious suite, the frog says, "Kiss me!"

The man complies, and the frog changes into a beautiful young girl.

At his hearing he tells the judge the whole story, and explains, "And that, your honor, that's how I happened to have a sixteen-year-old girl in my room."

159. Dumb Blonde Joke #103

A blonde drove her car into the repair shop to get an estimate for removing a small dent in her left rear door. The foreman thinks he'll see how gullible she is and says, "I'd have to charge you $150. But you can repair it yourself."

"How can I do that?"

"When the engine cools down, just blow into the tailpipe, and it should pop right out," he replies.

She thanks him and drives back to her home; when the engine cools, the blonde proceeds to blow into the tailpipe.

Her friend, another blonde, comes upon the scene and questions, "What in the world are you doing?"

The first blonde explains the situation.

Her friend explodes, "You're the type of blonde that gives the rest of us a bad reputation. How could you possibly expect that to work? Don't you realize you have to roll up the windows first?"

160. The Guide Dog

A blind man and his guide dog approach a busy intersection with a traffic light. The dog starts across the street against the traffic.

Another man, waiting for the light to change, grabs the blind man's arm, and warns him about the dog's error.

The man reaches into his pocket and pulls out a dog treat.

"Gosh, how understanding you are to give a treat to your dog when he might have killed you," observes the rescuer.

"I'm giving him the treat so I can find out where his head is, and then I can kick him in the ass."

161. Regularity

A reporter is interviewing a 104-year-old man. "Sir, to what do you attribute your longevity?"

"Regularity!" the old man quickly responds. "I always eat breakfast at six-twenty, lunch at twelve, and dinner at five-thirty in the evening. I have a bowel movement promptly at five-thirty every morning. I urinate promptly at five-thirty-five. Unfortunately, I now wake up at six AM."

162. Sexual Differences between Men and Women

I have never quite determined why the sexual urge in men and women differs so much. I can't figure out why men think with their heads, and women with their hearts.

For example: One evening last week, my girlfriend and I were getting into bed. Well, the passion starts to heat up, and she eventually says, "I don't feel like it. I just want you to hold me."

I said, "What? What? What was that you said?"

So, she says the words that every boyfriend or husband on the planet dreads to hear: "You're just not in touch enough with my emotional needs as a woman for me to satisfy your physical needs as a man." She responded to my puzzled look by saying, "Can't you just love me for who I am, and not what I do for you in the bedroom?"

Realizing nothing was going to happen tonight, I went to sleep.

The very next day I opted to take the day off from work to spend time with her. We went out to lunch and then went shopping at an exclusive department store. I walked along with her as she tried on several different and very expensive outfits. She couldn't decide on which one to take, so I told her we'd just buy them all. She wanted new shoes to complement her new clothes, so I told her to get a pair for each outfit. Next, we went to the jewelry department where she picked out a pair of diamond earrings. Let me tell you, she was so excited, she must have thought I'd struck it rich at the track. I started to think she was testing me because she asked for a tennis bracelet when she didn't know how to play tennis.

I think I threw her for a loop when I said, "I think that's fine, honey."

She was almost nearing sexual satisfaction from all the excitement. Smiling with excited anticipation, she finally said, "I think this is all, dear. Let's go to the cashier."

I could hardly contain myself when I blurted out, "No, honey, I don't feel like it!"

Her face just went completely blank as her jaw dropped with a baffled "WHAT?"

Then I said, "Honey, I just want you to hold this stuff for awhile. You're not in touch with my financial needs as a man enough for me to satisfy your shopping needs as a woman." And, just when she had this look like she would kill me, I added, "Why can't you just love me for who I am, and not for the things I can buy you?"

Apparently, I'm not having sex tonight, either.

163. Involuntary Muscular Contractions

A professor at the school of medicine was giving a lecture on "Involuntary Muscular Contractions" to his first-year medical students. Realizing this was not the most riveting subject, the professor decided to liven things up a bit. He pointed to a young woman in the front row and said, "Do you know what your asshole is doing while you're having an orgasm?"

She replied, "Probably deer hunting with his buddies!"

164. IRS Audits Grandpa

The IRS decided to audit Grandpa and summoned him to their office.

The auditor was not surprised when Grandpa showed up with his attorney.

The auditor explains, "Well, sir, you have an extravagant lifestyle and no full-time employment. You explain this circumstance by saying you win money gambling. I'm not sure the IRS finds that believable."

"I'm a great gambler, and I can prove it," says Gramps. "how about a demonstration?"

The auditor thinks for a moment, then says, "Okay, go ahead."

Granddad declares, "I'll bet you a thousand dollars that I can bite my own eye."

The auditor hesitates, and then finally replies, "It's a bet."

Grandpa removes his glass eye and bites it. The auditor's jaw drops.

Grandpa smiles and says, "Now, I'll bet you two thousand dollars I can bite my other eye."

The auditor can tell Grandpa isn't blind, so he takes the bet.

Granddad removes his dentures and bites his good eye.

The stunned auditor now realizes he has wagered and lost three grand, with Grandpa's attorney as a witness. He starts to get nervous.

"Want to go double or nothing?" Grandpa asks. "I'll bet you six thousand dollars I can stand on one side of your desk, and pee into that wastebasket on the other side, and never get a drop in-between."

The auditor, twice-burned, is cautious now, but he looks carefully and decides there is no way the old guy could manage this stunt, so he agrees.

Grandpa stands beside the desk and unzips his pants. Although he strains mightily, he can't make the stream reach the wastebasket, so he pretty well urinates all over the auditor's desk.

The auditor leaps for joy, realizing that he has just turned a major loss into a huge win.

But Grandfather's attorney moans and puts his head between his hands.

"Are you OK?" the auditor asks.

"Not really," says the attorney. "This morning, when Grandpa told me he was summoned for an audit, he bet me twenty-five thousand dollars that he could come in here and piss all over your desk, and that you'd be happy about it."

(My grandfather told me that if someone came up to me and bet five bucks a worm would come out of an apple waving an American flag, to be prepared to salute.)

165. A Tradition Is Born

This is a Christmas story for people having a bad day.

The day before Christmas, four of Santa's elves got sick, and the trainee elves did not produce toys fast enough. Santa began to feel the pre-Christmas pressure.

Then Mrs. Claus told Santa her mother was coming to visit, which stressed Santa even more.

When he went out to harness the reindeer, he found that three of them were about to give birth, and two others had jumped the fence and were out, Heaven knows where. As he began to load the sleigh, one of the runners broke, the toy bag fell out, and all the toys were scattered.

Thoroughly frustrated, Santa went into the house for a cup of cider and a shot of rum. When he opened the cupboard he found the elves had drunk all the cider, and hidden the liquor. In his frustration, Santa accidentally dropped the cider jug, and it broke into hundreds of pieces all over the kitchen floor. He went to get a broom, and found the mice had eaten all the straw off the bottom of the broom.

Just then, the doorbell rang. Irritated beyond belief, Santa yanked the door open. There stood a little angel with a huge Christmas tree.

The angel said, very cheerfully, "Merry Christmas, Santa. Isn't this a lovely day? I have a beautiful tree for you. Where would you like me to stick it?"

Thus began the tradition of the little angel on top of the Christmas tree.

166. The Bad-mouthed Parrot

A young man, named John, received a parrot as a gift.

The parrot proved to have a bad attitude, and an even worse vocabulary. Every word out of the bird's mouth was either rude, obnoxious, or laced with profanity.

John tried and tried to change the bird's attitude by consistently saying only polite words, playing soft music, and anything else he could think of to clean up the bird's demeanor and vocabulary.

Finally, John was fed up, and he yelled at the parrot. The parrot yelled back. He shook the parrot, and the bird got angrier and ruder. In desperation, John grabbed the bird from its perch, and put him in the freezer.

For a few minutes the bird squawked, kicked, and screamed. Then, suddenly, there was total quiet. Not a peep was heard for over a minute. Fearing he might have hurt the bird, John opened the freezer door.

The parrot calmly stepped out onto John's extended hand and said, "I believe I may have offended you with my rude language and actions. I am sincerely remorseful for my inappropriate transgressions, and I fully intend to do everything I can to correct my rude and unforgivable behavior."

John was stunned at the remarkable change in the bird's behavior, and the sincerity of its apology.

As he was about to ask the parrot what had brought about such a dramatic change, the bird inquired, "May I ask what the turkey did?"

167. The Service Charge

Billy Bob was home alone on the farm, when their neighbor, Mr. Jenkins, knocked on the door. Billy Bob answered the door, and asked farmer Jenkins if he could help hm.

"I really would like to talk to your daddy."

"I'm sorry," the boy replied. "Daddy's gone to town and won't be back til late afternoon."

"Then, I'd like to speak to your mama," Mr. Jenkins said.

"Mama went to town with daddy. Are you sure I can't help you?" the boy inquired. "I know most of what goes on on our farm."

"You tell your daddy I'd like to speak to him about your brother Ralph getting my daughter, Mary Belle, pregnant."

"Well, I know daddy charges $50 for the bull, and $35 for the boar, but I don't know how much he charges for Ralph."

168. Blind Man in a Blonde Bar

A blind man walking down the street smells the scent of beer. He enters the bar and orders a beer. "Dies anyone want to hear a blonde joke?" he asks.

A woman says, "I know you're blind. So let me warn you: this is a blonde bar. I am the owner, and I'm blonde. The bartender is a blonde; the woman on your right is a blonde, weighs 200 pounds, and is an Olympic weight-lifter; the woman on your left weighs 220 pounds, and is a professional wrestler."

The owner asks, "Now, do you still want to tell your blonde joke?"

"Nah, not if I have to explain it four times."

169. Forgetful

A man and his wife were driving on a long trip. They decide to stop at a roadside restaurant for lunch.

After their meal, about twenty miles beyond the restaurant, the wife says, "Bill, turn around. I left my sweater on the back of the chair."

"We're on a Turnpike; there won't be a turnoff for another fifteen miles. You're so forgetful. This is going to throw us off schedule a full hour."

Bill continues his tirade until they returned to the restaurant. As his wife steps out of the car, Bill calls, in a sweet voice, "Honey, when you pick up your sweater, will you get my credit card from the cashier, and the hat I left in our booth?"

170. The Barber Shop

One day a man pokes his head into a barber shop and asks the owner, "How long before I can get a haircut?"

The barber looks around and observes, "It looks like about an hour and a half."

"Thanks," says the fellow, and closes the door.

About a week later the same man opens the barber shop door and inquires, "How long to get my hair cut?"

The owner answers, "About forty-five minutes."

"Thanks," says the man, as he closes the door, and leaves.

The same thing happens the following week. The man asks how long before he could get a haircut. The barber, somewhat exasperated, declares, "Maybe an hour."

As usual, the man leaves. The barber asks one of his regular patrons to follow the guy and report where he went.

A few minutes later the patron returns, chuckling.

"Well," asks the barber, "where did he go?"

The client replies, "Your house!"

171. Telling the Sex of Flies

A woman came home to see her husband in the kitchen with a fly swatter, killing flies.

"Were there many flies, honey?" she asked.

"I caught five—two female and three male."

"How can you tell the sex of a fly?"

"There were two on the telephone, and three on the beer can."

172. The Prenuptial Agreement

An elderly couple decides to get married, and are preparingtheir prenuptial agreement.

The woman says, "I want to keep my house."

Her intended replies, "I can agree with that."

She then says, "I want to keep my Rolls-Royce."

Again, he agrees.

"Next," she demands, "I want to have sex seven days a week."

The old man replies, "I can agree to that. Put me down for Thursdays."

173. Catholic Wisdom

The 98-year-old, Irish-born, Mother Superior of St. Mary's Convent is dying.

The nuns gather around her bed, trying to make her last journey comfortable. They try giving her some warm milk to drink, but she refuses it.

One of the nuns takes the glass back to the kitchen, and, remembering a bottle of Irish whisky received the previous Christmas, opens the bottle; she pours a generous amount into the warm milk.

Back at the Mother Superior's bed, she holds the glass to her lips. The Mother drinks a little, then a little more. Before they know it, she has consumed the whole glass.

"Mother," the nuns ask earnestly, "please gives us some wisdom before you die."

She raises herself up in the bed and says, "DON'T SELL THAT COW!"

174. Married in Haste

A man meets a most beautiful woman. They seemed to hit it off immediately, and he suggests they get married that day, claiming they will get to know each other over time.

The woman agrees.

On their honeymoon, at the hotel's pool, the man gets up and climbs the ten—meter board, and jumps off into a 2½ twist, with three rotations in the pike position, straightens out, and enters the water like a knife. He completes several dives to an appreciative crowd.

His new wife is impressed. "That was magnificent! Where did you learn to dive so professionally?"

"I told you we'd get to know each other over time," he replies. "I was an Olympic Diving Champion."

His new wife gets up and dives into the pool. After 30 laps in the 50 meter pool, she emerges, hardly out of breath.

"You must have been an Olympic endurance swimmer," her husband comments.

"No, I was a prostitute from St. Louis, and worked both sides of the Mississippi."

175. Ten Dollars Is Ten Dollars

At a carnival in the early thirties, an old farmer was desirous of taking a plane ride in an open-cockpit aircraft.

His wife was dead-set against it, saying, "Ten dollars is ten dollars, and we can't afford it."

The pilot overheard their conversation and said, "I'll take both of you up for free, provided neither of you say a word during the flight." He was sure his aerobatics would elicit some screams.

They took off, and the pilot did every scary maneuver he could, but there wasn't a peep from the rear cockpit. After ten minutes he landed the plane, and was astounded to find the woman was gone. "What happened to your wife?" he asked.

The old man replied, "She fell out when you made the first loop."

"Good God, man, why didn't you tell me?"

"Well, ten dollars is ten dollars."

176. Why Parents Get Old

When his employee fails to show up for work, the boss calls the man's home.

A child answers, whispering, "Hello."

The boss asks, "May I speak with your father?"

"No, sir," the child states.

"Then let me speak to your mother."

"No," replies the child. "They are both talking to the police and firemen."

Just then the boss hears a roar over the phone. "What was that?" he asks.

"That's the hellingcopter, with the search team."

"What are they searching for?" inquires the boss.

"Me," giggles the child.

177. Wally's Wedding Night

It was Wally's wedding night; he's 85, and she's 28. They decided on separate rooms to keep from exhausting the old man.

At ten o'clock, the girl hears a knock on the door; it's Wally. They make love, and then Wally retires to his room.

At midnight, the girl awakens to a knock on her door; it's Wally again. They copulate a second time and Wally retires.

At three A.M., he awakens his wife again. She says, "You are the greatest lover ever. You're more virile than anyone half your age."

Wally inquires, "Do you mean I was here before?"

178. Forced to Go to Church

One Sunday morning, a mother goes into her son's room to tell him it is time to get ready for church, to which he replies, "I'm not going."

"Why not?" his mother asks.

"I'll give you two reasons," he says. "One, they don't like me, and two, I don't like them."

His mother responds, "I'll give you two reasons why you should go to church. One, you're 59 years old, and two, you're the priest."

179. Close the Garage Door

The boss walks into the office one morning not knowing his pants zipper is down and his fly is wide open. His assistant comes up to him and says, "This morning when you left your house, did you close your garage door?"

The boss knew he had closed the garage door, and walks into his office with a puzzled look on his face. As he finishes his paperwork, he suddenly notices his fly is open, and he zips it up. He then understood his assistant's question about the garage door.

He heads out for a cup of coffee, and, as he passes by her desk, he asks, "When my garage door was open, did you see my Hummer?"

She smiles and replies, "No. All I saw was the old version of the Mini-Cooper with two flat tires."

180. Tickle Me Elmo

There is a factory in Minnesota that makes the Tickle Me Elmo toys. The toy laughs when you tickle it under the arms.

Lena was hired at the factory, and she reported for her first day at 8:00 AM.

The next day, at 8:45 AM, there was a knock on the Personnel Manager's door. The foreman throws open the door, and begins to rant about the new employee.

He complains she's incredibly slow, and the whole production line is being held up.

The Personnel Manager decides he should see for himself, so the two men march down to the factory floor. When they get there the line is so backed up there are Tickle Me Elmos all over the floor, and they're really piling up.

At the end of the line stands Lena, surrounded by mountains of Tickle Me Elmos. She has a roll of plush red fabric and a huge bag of marbles.

The two men stare in amazement as she cuts a little piece of fabric, wraps it around two marbles, and then begins to sew the little package between Elmo's legs.

The Manager bursts into laughter. After several seconds of hysterics he pulls himself together and the two men approach Lena.

"I'm sorry," he says to her, barely able to keep a straight face, "but you misunderstood the directions I gave you yesterday. Your job is to give Elmo two test tickles."

181. The Church's Usher

An elderly woman walks into the local country church. A friendly usher greets her at the door and helps her up the steps into the chapel. "Where would you like to sit?" he asks.

"The front row, please."

"You really don't want to do that," the usher says. "The pastor is really boring."

"Do you happen to know who I am?" the woman demands.

"No, ma'am," he replies.

"I'm the pastor's mother," she declares indignantly.

"Do you know who I am?" he asks.

"No," she answers.

"Good," he responds.

182. The Twenty and the One

A well-worn dollar bill and a similarly distressed twenty-dollar bill arrived at a Federal Reserve Bank to be retired. As they moved along the conveyor belt to be burned, they struck up a conversation.

The twenty-dollar bill reminisced about his travels all over the country. "I've had a pretty good life," the twenty proclaimed. "I've been to Las Vegas and Atlantic City, the finest restaurants in New York, performances on Broadway, and even a cruise to the Caribbean."

"Wow," said the dollar bill. "You've really had an exciting life!"

"So tell me," said the twenty, "where have you been throughout your lifetime?"

The dollar bill replies, "Oh, I've been to the Methodist Church, the Baptist Church, the Lutheran Church, and . . ."

The twenty-dollar bill interrupts. "What's a church?"

183. The Frog

At Show-and-Tell time at the local elementary school, Tommy Jones stood up and said, "I found a dead frog on the way to school today."

The teacher inquired, "How did you know it was dead, Tommy?"

"I pissed in its ear."

"YOU DID WHAT?"

"You know, I bent down and went 'psssst' in its ear, and it didn't move."

184. The Blond Cowboy

Sheriff Tom was driving up Main Street, when he was surprised to see Billy-Bob Stover walking in the middle of the road, stark naked, except for his boots and Stetson. The sheriff pulled up and ordered Billy-Bob to get in the back seat of his cruiser. "Billy-Bob, what the hell are you doin' walkin' into town naked as a jaybird?"

"Well, sheriff. I was havin' a beer at the Lazy J Saloon when this purtty woman comes up to me and says, 'Cowboy, how'd you like to see my new motor-home?'"

"A course I said, 'Yes.' So we went into the parkin' lot and there was this beautiful, huge, motorhome."

"She unlocked the door and we went in. She took me back to the bedroom, which had a slide-out on both sides. She took off her blouse, and told me to take off my shirt. Which I did. Then she took off her skirt, and told me to take off my pants. Which I did.

"Then she took off her bra, and told me to take off my undershirt. Which I did. Then she slipped off her panties, and told me to take off my jockeys. Which I did. Then she climbs on the bed all sexy-like and says, 'Go to town, cowboy.'"

"Which I was."

185. Golf Leprechaun

An Irish golfer teed up his ball, swung, and watched his ball slice into the woods. He waded through the thicket of undergrowth and came to a clearing. There on the ground lay a leprechaun, a lump on his forehead, and the golfer's ball beside him. "Oh. Lord, what have I done?" he cried. A small stream wandered through the wood, so the man moistened his handkerchief and placed it on the leprechaun's head.

The little man woke up and said, "Ya caught me. I'll lead ya to me pot-o-gold."

"Oh, no," the golfer cried. "I am so sorry to have hurt you. You owe me nothing."

"Ya caught me, fair and square; I'm bound by our law to give ya the gold."

"No, I cannot accept it. I am happy you are feeling well after I hit you on the head. Again, I'm sorry I hurt you." With that, the golfer took his ball and went back to the golf course.

A year, to the day, after he had struck the leprechaun, the golfer again sliced his ball into the woods. This time, the leprechaun was sitting on a rock, with the golfer's golf ball in his hand. "And how are ya, my friend?" he asked.

"I'm fine."

"Tell me," said the leprechaun. "How's yer golf game?"

"Wonderful. I'm now shooting par, almost all the time."

"I gave ya that fer bein' such a good man. How's yer financial situation?"

"Oh, just wonderful. I seem to always make the right investments."

"I gave ya that, too. Tell me, how's yer sex life?"

"About twice a year."

"Twice a year? How can that be? I gave ya a healthy sex life."

"I don't think it's so bad for the priest in a small parish."

186. Japanese Short-sword Championship

A reporter arrived after the Japanese short-sword competition had been completed. Hoping to still get a story, he approached the third-place winner. "I apologize for being late. I missed your demonstration. Could you show me an example of your skills that enabled you to take third place?"

"Of course," the man replied. "You see fry on wall?"

"Yes, sir. I do."

"You watch, prease." The man stepped to the wall and blew on the fly, which immediately took off. With a flash of his sword, the fly fell to the floor, sliced perfectly in half, from head to tail.

"Most remarkable," said the reporter. "Thank you."

Stepping to the second-place competitor, he inquired, "I've interviewed the third-place winner, and was wondering how you were able to improve upon his performance."

"Prease to observe fry on wall," he instructed. He too blew on the fly, which flew away. In the blink of an eye his sword went swish, swish. The fly fell to the floor in quarters.

"Very impressive," remarked the reporter. "I can see why you took second place."

Moving to the winner of first place, he asked, "I have just witnessed the ability of the second-place contestant. I can't see how you could better his performance. Would you demonstrate your special skills that enabled you to achieve first place?"

The contest must have been conducted in an abandoned bakery, because the man said, "You see fry on wall?"

"Yes," said the reporter.

"You watch, prease." He leaned over and blew on the fly, which flew away. Swish, swish, swish, the sword moved at lightning speed. The fly continued to fly, landing on a table.

"I'm sorry, sir. The fly is still alive. I cannot understand what you accomplished that warrants first-place."

Handing the reporter a magnifying glass, the man replied, (Alternate punch-line #1) "You rook very crosery, and you find fry no longer aberr to make babies." (Alternate punch-line #2) "You rook very crosery, and you find fry is now Jewish."

187. Sexiest Italian Woman

Three Italians were arguing about who they'd want to be with on a deserted island.

The first picked Gina Lollobrigida. "She's the most beautiful woman in the world."

"I'd prefer Sophia Loren," said the second man. "She's the sexiest woman in the world."

They both looked at the third man. "Who would you like to be with?"

"Ima like Virginia Pip Eleenee. She wants sex all a time."

"Who's Virginia Pip Eleenee?" they ask.

"I don no, but she's a in a newspaper; see."

The headline said: "Two hundred lay Virginia Pipeline in three days."

188. Incorrigible Johnny

"Mom," Johnny asks, "can I have a bike for Christmas?"

"I don't know, Johnny. Why don't you write a letter to the Blessed Virgin Mother Mary? She may convince Santa Claus to give you one."

John sat down at the desk and began to write, "Dear Blessed Virgin Mother Mary, I have been a very good boy . . ." Knowing this to be untrue, he tossed the first letter away, and began to compose another. "Dear Blessed Virgin Mother Mary, I have been pretty good . . ." Again, he scrapped the letter. Pulling out a fresh sheet, he began, "Dear Blessed Virgin Mother Mary, I have tried to be a good . . ." His conscience got the better of him and he threw the letter away.

A crafty smile creased his face and he went to the Christmas Manger scene under the tree, took the Christ-child figure, and placed it in his sock drawer. Again he started writing a letter. "Dear Blessed Virgin Mother Mary, if you ever want to see your child again . . ."

189. Evolution vs. Creation

A young girl asked her mother, "Mom, how did people come to be?"

The mother replied, "God created Adam and Eve, and they had children."

The girl queried her father, "Daddy, how did people come to be?"

Her father answered, "Many centuries ago, there were monkeys, and we descended from them."

Perplexed, the girl went back to her mother and said, "You told me God created Adam and Eve and we descended from them. Daddy said we descended from monkeys."

"Dear," her mother responded, "I was talking about my side of the family; he was talking about his."

190. New Hearing-aids

An elderly gentleman had serious hearing deficiencies for many years. Finally he consulted an audiologist who was able to fit him for a set of hearing aids that allowed the gentleman to hear 100%.

The man came back in a month for a checkup, and the doctor said, "You're hearing is perfect. Your family must be really pleased you can hear again."

The gentleman replied, "Oh, I haven't told my family yet."

"Why not?" asked the doctor.

"I just sit around and listen to their conversations. I've changed my will three times."

191. Mexican Rocky Mountain Oysters

An American, vacationing in Mexico City, had just been seated in the hotel's dining room. He was consulting the menu when he noticed the waiter bringing a sizzling, sumptuous dinner to a patron at the next table. Not only did it look good, the smell was wonderful. It contained two of the biggest Rocky Mountain Oysters the man had ever seen, smothered in a savory-appearing sauce. When his waiter appeared, the American said, "I'll have what that man ordered."

The waiter replied, "Ah, Senor. You have excellent taste! Those are called Cojones de Toro, bull's testicles from the bull killed today in the main event at the bull-ring. It is a delicacy!"

"They look delicious," said the American. "Please bring me an order."

The waiter replied, "I am sorry, Senor; that is a special order, and we can only serve one order each day."

"May I order the dish for tomorrow night?" inquired the American.

"Of course, Senor, we will have it prepared especially for you."

The next evening the American appeared at the dining room and was escorted to his table.

Soon a waiter appeared, holding the plate high above his head. With a flourish, he set it down. The American was appalled at the pullet-egg-sized testicles, and said to the waiter, "Last night you served magnificent testicles; today, you serve little ones. Why?"

The waiter shrugged his shoulders and replied, "Senor, sometimes the bull, he wins!"

192. Difference between Grandpas and Grandmas

A man who worked away from home all week, always made a special effort to be with his family on weekends. Every Sunday morning he would take his seven-year-old granddaughter out for a drive in the car for some bonding time; just him and his granddaughter.

One particular Sunday, however, he had a bad cold, and really didn't feel like being up at all. Luckily, his wife came to the rescue and said she would take their granddaughter out for a drive.

When they returned, the little girl anxiously ran upstairs to see her grandfather.

"Well, did you enjoy your ride with grandma?" he asked.

"Oh yes, Papa." the girl replied, "And did you know what? We didn't see a single dumb bastard or lousy shithead anywhere we went today!"

193. The Man of the House

A man had just finished reading a new book, entitled *You Can Be the Man of Your House.*

He storms into the kitchen, and says to his wife, "From now on you need to know that I am the man of this house, and my word is law. You will prepare me a gourmet meal tonight, and when I'm finished eating my meal, you will serve me a sumptuous desert. After dinner, you are going upstairs with me and we will have the kind of sex I want.

"Afterwards, you are going to draw me a bath so I can relax. You will wash my back, towel me dry, and bring me my robe. Next, you will massage my feet and hands.

"Then, tomorrow, guess who's going to dress me and comb my hair?"

The wife replies, "The funeral director would be my first guess."

194. Give Me a Clue

An elderly couple had dinner at another couple's house. After dinner, the wives left the table and went into the kitchen.

The two gentlemen were talking, when one says, "Last night we went out to a new restaurant and it was great. I recommend it very highly."

The other man inquires, "What's its name?"

The first man thought for a moment and finally says, "What's the name of the flower you give to someone you love? You know, it's red and has thorns."

The other man responds, "Do you mean a rose?"

"That's it." The man then turned to the kitchen and yelled, "Rose, what's the name of the restaurant we went to last night?"

195. How to Get Your Wife Pregnant

Rex Armstrong had the body of an Olympic swimmer—broad shoulders, narrow waist, well-defined abs, strong legs and arms. His neighbor, Charlie, was more of the Casper Milquetoast type—slim, to the point of being skinny; receding chin; five-foot-six—a typical weakling.

One day, the men were working in their backyards, when Rex calls Charlie over to the fence. "Charlie," he says, "we've lived next door to one another for six years. We were both newlyweds, but you have five children, while Phyllis and I have none. Is there some secret you could share with me as to how I can get her pregnant?"

"Yes, Rex. First, you have to move your bed so it points true north; head north, feet south. Then put clean sheets on the bed. Sprinkle a little fragrance onto the sheets to make them smell nice. Next, draw a nice warm bath for Phyllis, with some bubble-bath crystals. Don't let her do any work. You pick her up, carry her into the bathroom, and place her gently in the water. Wash her all over, and then lift her out of the tub. Remember: don't let her do any work. Pat her dry with a towel and dust her with sweet-smelling powder. Pick her up and carry her into the bedroom, and place her on the bed—head north, feet south.

"Then call me on the phone, and I'll be right over."

196. Not Quite the Same Thing

On her eighteenth birthday, a young black girl comes down for breakfast all dressed up, and carrying a suitcase.

"Where ya'll goin, honey?" her mother asks.

"My boyfriend, Leroy, said he was goin to take me to Florida on my eighteenth birthday."

"What a fine boy to give ya'll such a nice present. Ya'll have a good time."

The girl walks down to the corner garage where her boyfriend works. He rolls out from under a car and asks. "Where ya'll goin, honey?"

"Does ya'll mean you forgot? Ya'll said on my eighteenth birthday ya was goin to take me to Florida."

"Honey," he replies. "Ya'll misunderstood me. I said when ya got to be eighteen, I was gonna tampa with ya."

197. Go Fly a Kite

A husband is in his backyard attempting to fly a kite. He lays the kite on the ground, pays out some string, then runs to the side of the yard. The wind would catch it for a moment, then the kite would start to spin and crash to the ground. He tries this several times, always with the same result.

All the while, his wife is watching from the kitchen window. She mutters to herself how men need to be told how to do everything. She opens the window and shouts, "You need a piece of tail."

The man turns with a confused look on his face and says, "Make up your mind. Last night you told me to go fly a kite."

198. Daddy's Home

A man calls his home and a little girl answers, "Hello."

"Hi, honey, this is Daddy. Would you please tell Mommy I'd like to talk to her?"

"I can't," says the girl.

"Why not, dear?"

"She's in the bedroom with Uncle Frank."

"You have an Uncle Frank?"

"That's what Mommy calls him."

"Dear, do me a favor and go into the hall and yell to Mommy that Daddy's home. Then tell me what happens."

"Yes, Daddy." A few moments later she returned to the phone. "I did what you told me, Daddy."

"What happened?" asks her father.

"Mommy came out of the bedroom and tripped while she was putting on her sweat pants. She fell down the stairs and I think she broke her neck."

"What happened to Uncle Frank?" he inquires.

"He jumped out the bedroom window into the swimming pool. I guess he forgot you drained it."

The man thought for a moment. "Swimming pool? Is this 555-1247?"

199. The Cell Phone

After their golf game, several men were relaxing in the club sauna. The melodious tone of a cell phone interrupted their conversation.

One of the men picked up the phone and spoke, "Hello."

"Hi, dear," said a woman's voice. "Where are you?"

"In the club's sauna," he replied.

"I'm glad I found you," the woman continued. "The Mercedes dealer called and said he just received the silver convertible I wanted. He said the price was $75,950."

"He's way over price. Tell him you'll give him $69,250 and not a penny more. Also, demand free service for 5,000 miles. I'm pretty sure he'll accept the offer."

"Oh, darling, thank you so much," the woman replies. "While you're in such a generous mood, the chinchilla coat I wanted has been reduced from $12,000, to $7,300. Can we afford it?"

"That sounds more reasonable. Go buy it, but tell them you want free cold storage."

"Dearest, you're wonderful. I don't want to press my luck, but the villa on the French Riviera we stayed at last year, is up for sale. The realtor called, and said we could buy it for $360,000."

"Too much," the man answers. "With the economy failing in France, he'll settle for less. Offer him $320,000."

"Lover," the woman enthused, "you're going to get very lucky tonight. I love you. Goodbye."

The man closed up the phone, held it up, and asked, "Anyone know whose cell phone this is?"

200. Dumb Blonde Joke #223

A group of women are playing a game of Trivial Pursuit. A blonde's token has landed on Science and Technology. Her question is, "You're in a vacuum. Can you hear any sound?"

The blonde asks, "Is it on or off?"

201. Mathematical Problem

A boss asks his secretary, "If I gave you 14% of $20,000, how much would you take off?"

She replied, "Everything, except my earrings."

202. A True Texas Lady

A very gentle Texas lady is driving across a high bridge in Texas. As she nears the top she notices a young man fixin (means "getting ready" in Texan) to jump. She stops her car, rolls down the window, and says, "Please don't jump. Think of your dear mother and father."

He answers, "Mom and Dad are both dead. I'm going to jump."

She replies, "Well, think of your wife and children."

"I'm not married, and I don't have children."

She says, "Well, then, 'Remember the Alamo.'"

He replies, "What's the Alamo?"

She declares, "Well, bless your heart, just go right ahead and jump, you dumb-ass Yankee."

203. John's Robot

John was a salesman's delight when it came to any kind of unusual gimmick.

His wife, Marsha, had long ago given up trying to get him to change. One day John came home with another one of his unconventional purchases. It was a robot that John claimed was a lie detector.

It was about 5:30 in the afternoon when Tim, their eleven-year-old son, returned home from school. Timmy was over two hours late. "Sit down, son," John instructed. "Now, tell us where you've been? Why are you late coming home?"

"Several of us went to the library to work on an extra credit project," replied Timmy. The robot walked around the table and slapped Tim, knocking him completely out of the chair.

"Son," said John, "this robot is a lie detector. Now, tell us where you really were after school."

"We went to Bobby's house and watched a movie," Tim answered.

"What did you watch?" asked Marsha.

"The Ten Commandments," Timmy answered.

The robot went around and once again slapped him. With his lip quivering, Timmy cried, "I'm sorry. I lied. We really watched a tape called *Sex Queen*."

"I'm ashamed of you, son," his dad replied. "When I was your age, I never lied to my parents."

The robot walked around to John and delivered a whack that nearly knocked him off his feet.

Marsha doubled over with laughter, almost in tears, and said, "Boy, did you ever ask for that one. You can't be too hard on Timmy. After all, he is your son."

The robot walked over to Marsha and knocked her out of her chair.

204. In These Depressed Times

Two car salesmen are sitting at a bar. One complains to the other, "Boy, business stinks. If I don't sell more cars this month, I'm going to lose my ass."

He then notices a beautiful blonde two stools away. Immediately, he apologizes for his bad language.

"That's okay," the blonde replies, "I can relate; if I don't sell more ass this month, I'm going to lose my car."

205. Dumb Blonde Joke #4

A blonde comes home early from shopping and hears strange noises coming from the bedroom.

She rushes upstairs, only to find her husband naked, lying on the bed, sweating and panting.

"What's up?" she asks.

"I think I'm having a heart attack," cries her husband.

The blonde grabs the bedside phone, but as she's dialing, her four-year-old son comes up and says, "Mommy! Mommy! Aunty Shirley is hiding in your closet, and she has no clothes on."

The blonde slams the phone down and storms past her husband, and rips open the closet door. Sure enough, there's her sister cowering on the floor.

"You rotten 'bitch,'" she screams. "My husband's having a heart attack, and you're running around naked playing hide-and-seek with the kids!"

206. As Long as It's Good for Business

A fellow tours a factory that produces latex products. At the first stop, he's shown the machine which manufactures baby-bottle nipples. The machine makes a loud hiss-pop noise. The guide explains, "The hiss is the rubber being injected into the mold.

The popping sound is the needle poking a hole in the end of the nipple."

Later, the tour reaches the part of the factory where condoms are made. The machine makes a hiss, hiss, hiss, hiss-pop, sound.

"Wait a minute," says the man taking the tour. "I understand what the hiss is, but what's that pop every so often?"

"Oh, it's the same as the baby-bottle nipple machine," says the guide. "It pokes a hole in every fourth condom."

"Well," replies the man, "that can't be good for the condom."

The guide answers, "No, but it's great for the baby-bottle nipple business."

207. Balance

God was missing for six days. Eventually, Michael, the Archangel, found him, resting on the seventh day.

Michael inquired, "Where have you been?"

God smiled proudly, and pointed down through the clouds. "Look, Michael. Look what I've made."

The Archangel looked puzzled, and asked, "What is it?"

"It's a planet," God replied, "and I put life on it. I'm calling it Earth, and it's going to be a place to test balance."

"Balance?" queried Michael. "I'm confused."

God explained, pointing to different parts of the earth. "For example, northern Europe will be a place of great opportunity and wealth, while southern Europe is going to be poor. Over here I've placed a continent of white people, and over there is a continent of black people. Balance in all things."

God continued pointing to different countries. "This one will be extremely hot, while this one will be very cold and covered with ice."

The Archangel, impressed with God's work, pointed to a land area and said, "What's that one?"

"That's Washington State, the most glorious place on earth. There are beautiful mountains, rivers, and streams, lakes, forests, hills, and plains. The people of Washington State are going to be handsome, modest, intelligent, and humorous, and they are going to travel the world. They will be extremely sociable, hardworking, high-achieving, carriers of peace and producers of software."

Michael gasped in wonder and admiration, but then asked, "But what about balance, God? You said there would be balance."

God smiled. "There's another Washington. Wait till you see the idiots I'll put there!"

208. Just Twenty-four Hours to Live

Morris returns from the doctor's office, and tell his wife that he has just twenty-four hours to live.

"Darling," Morris asks, "could we have sex?"

"Certainly, dear," she replies. "Any time you want. It is the least I can do for you."

About six hours later, Morris asks, "Sweetheart, I now have eighteen hours left. Could we make love again?"

"Of course, dear. Come into the bedroom with me."

Later, as they get ready for bed that night, Morris realizes he has only eight hours left on this world. He touches his wife's shoulder and asks, "Honey, please, just one more time before I die."

She agrees, and they make love for the third time.

After this session, the wife rolls over and falls asleep.

Morris, worried about his impending death, tosses and turns until he has just four hours left.

He taps his wife, who rouses. "Honey, I have only four more hours. Could we make love again?"

At this point the wife sits up in bed and says, "Listen, Morris, enough is enough. I have to get up in the morning—you don't."

209. Don't Ask Retired People Dumb Questions

Yesterday I was at my local COSTCO buying a large bag of Purina Dog Chow for my loyal pet Biscuit, and was in the checkout line when a woman asked me if I had a dog.

What did she think the dog food was for—an elephant? Since I am retired and take my entertainment when the opportunity presents itself, on impulse I told her, "No, I don't have a dog. I'm starting the Purina Diet again." I added that I probably shouldn't, because I ended up in the hospital the last time, but I had lost forty-two pounds before I awakened in the emergency ward with tubes coming out of nearly every orifice and IVs in both arms.

I told her that it was essentially a perfect diet, and the way it worked is to load your pockets with Purina nuggets and simply eat a couple every time you felt hungry. I explained that the food is nutritionally complete, so it works well, and I was going to try it again. (I should mention that practically everyone in line was enthralled with my story.)

Horrified, the woman asked if I had ended up in intensive care because the dog food had poisoned me.

I told her no, that I had stepped off the curb to sniff a poodle's butt and a car hit us both.

COSTCO won't let me shop there anymore.

210. Surprise

Dave was attending his hunting club's monthly meeting and had just told the members he couldn't make the hunting trip scheduled for the next day because his wife wouldn't let him go.

After listening to the jeers and other derisive remarks from his fellow hunting buddies, Dave left the meeting and went home to his wife.

The next day, when Dave's friends arrived to set up camp, who should be there but Dave, sitting in front of his tent, beer in hand, camp-oven roast broiling away in a hot bed of coals.

"How did you talk your wife into letting you come, Dave?"

"I didn't have to," was Dave's answer. "When I left the meeting I went home and slumped down in my chair with a beer to drown my sorrows. Then my wife snuck up behind me, covered my eyes, and said, 'Surprise!'

"When I peeled her hands back she was standing there in a beautiful see-through negligee and said, 'Carry me into the bedroom, tie me to the bed, and you can do whatever you want.'

"SO HERE I AM!"

211. The Practical Genie

A woman walking along the beach found an antique lamp. As she brushed the sand from its surface, out popped a Genie.

Surprised, she asked if she got three wishes, like in the storybooks.

The Genie answered, "Lady, three-wish genies are a myth. I'm just a one-wish genie. So, what'll it be?"

Without hesitation she replied, "I want peace in the Middle East. It's just awful over there, and it's affecting the entire world.

See this map? I want these three countries to stop fighting with each other. I want you to make the Arabs love the Jews and Americans, and vice versa. That will bring about world peace and harmony."

The genie looked at the map, and exclaimed, "Lady, be reasonable. These countries have been fighting each other for thousands of years. I've been in that lamp for 500 years, and I'm a bit out-of-shape. I'm good, but not that good. I don't think it can be done. Make another wish, and please try to make it simpler."

The woman thought for a moment and said, "Well, I've never been able to find the right man. You know, one who's considerate, fun, romantic, likes to cook and help around the house, is good in bed, can get along with my family, and is faithful. That's what I wish for—the perfect man."

The genie rolled his eyes, and said, "Gimme that friggin map!"

212. Sports Repairman

Three women were extolling the success of their sons.

The first said, "My Joey is a surgeon, He makes $400,000 a year and bought me a new Cadillac."

The second woman retorted, "My Bill is an attorney. He makes $800,000 a year and bought me a new home."

The third woman exclaimed, "My Tony makes over a million dollars a year and bought me a villa on the Italian Riviera, and a chauffeured limousine."

"What does your son do to make so much money?" inquired the other two women.

"I don't really know," the woman replied. "I think he's a sports repairman. He fixes basketball games, football games, boxing matches . . ."

213. Cause of Death

Three recently deceased women were comparing the reasons for their death.

The first said, "I died of the big H."

The second replied, "Heart attack, huh? I died of the big C. That's cancer, and I was in pain for months."

The two looked at the third and inquired, "What did you die of, honey?"

"I died of the big G."

"What in heaven's name is the big G?" they asked.

"That's gonorrhea."

"You don't die of gonorrhea," remarked one.

"You does if you gives it to Big Leroy!"

214. The Best Investment

A seventy-year-old Italian had given each of his sons $100,000. After twenty years, he summoned them to give an accounting as to how they spent their money.

"Father," said the eldest, "I used the money to put me through medical school. I am now a Board Certified surgeon, and make $500,000 a year."

"Thatsa good," said the old man. He motioned to his second son and inquired, "What did you do with the money I gave you?"

"Dad, I, too, invested in my education, and became an attorney. I make over a million dollars a year."

"Thatsa very good." He now looked at his youngest son, "You always been a lazy kid. What you do with my money?"

"Pop, I used the money to learn to be a magician."

"You no good kid! Wastea my money to be a magician!"

"No, Pop. I didn't waste it. Let me show you what I can do." With that, he waved his hand toward the television, and made a lifting motion with his hands. Slowly, the TV rose off its stand and hovered in the air. The young man clapped his hands and the TV settled back on its stand.

The old man, snorted, "So thatsa big nothing. What good does it do to make you money?"

The son then waved his hands at his two brothers, and lifted them into the air. He clapped his hands and they returned to the floor.

The old man was still not impressed. So the boy went up to his father and motioned at his crotch to rise. In a second, the old man had an erection, and cried, "Please. No clappa de hands. No clappa de hands. Take me to your mama."

215. Sex Survey

The lecturer remarked, "Before we get started on the topic, 'Sexuality Differences between Married Couples,' I'd like to take a short survey. How many of you have sex at least three times a week?"

A large number of his audience raises their hands.

"Okay. Now, how many of you have sex no more than once a week?"

Again, a large group raises their hands.

He then asks, "How many of you only have sex once a month?"

A few raise their hands.

"Is there anyone here who has sex less than once a month?"

One man raises his hand.

The lecturer inquires, "You seem to be very happy for someone having sex less than once a month."

The fellow replies, "Tonight's the night."

216. The Man, the Boy, and the Donkey

An old man and a young boy were leading a donkey through town, and the people said, "How stupid. The man and boy are walking when they have a perfectly good donkey to carry them."

After they had passed through the town, the man and boy climbed onto the donkey's back.

When they came to the next town, the people remarked, "Look at that inconsiderate young boy making the poor donkey carry two people when he's perfectly able to walk."

When they left the town, the boy got off and led the donkey while the old man rode. When they entered the next town, the people gasped and said, "Look at that old man riding that poor old donkey. You'd think he'd show more respect for the poor animal."

After they left the town, the old man carried the donkey on his shoulders. However, as they crossed a bridge, the old man stumbled, and the donkey plunged over the bridge and into the river.

The moral of the story is: If you try to please everyone, you'll lose your ass!

217. A Unique Change Purse

For years, a man has climbed aboard a Chicago streetcar every morning promptly at eight o'clock. He always pulls out a peculiar change purse from his pants pocket, opens it, and extracts six cents.

One day, the conductor summons the courage to ask the man about his strange purse. "Sir, I have never seen a change purse like yours. Can you tell me where you got it?"

The man replied, "I'm a rabbi. It is very special. I had it made from foreskins. If you rub it like this—surprise, it becomes a briefcase."

218. Quite a Bit of Difference

How do you tell the difference between a prostitute, a nymphomaniac, and a housewife?

A prostitute says, "Are YOU through?"

A nymphomaniac says, "ARE YOU THROUGH?"

A housewife says, "I think we should paint the ceiling blue."

219. Dumb Blonde Joke #222

A blonde entered the emergency room and complained that she ached all over.

The doctor asked her to show him where she hurt.

"When I touch my cheek, it hurts. When I touch my knee, it hurts. When I touch my hip, it hurts. What's my problem, doctor?"

He replied, "You have a broken finger."

220. Mercury Astronaut

A Mercury astronaut had been seated in the capsule for seven hours when ground control scrubbed the flight.

He went home and, a week later, was summoned for the next attempt. Again, after several hours waiting, the mission was scrubbed. He went home, and complained to his wife that there were so many problems with the missile he probably would never get his flight.

The next evening, he and his wife went out on the town. In the morning, he received a call from the base to report immediately to the launch pad.

His head was splitting, and he was seeing double. "Honey, would you please take my place?" he asked his wife. "I'm in no condition to fly. Besides, they'll just scrub the mission because of some failure. If, by some strange circumstance, they do launch, everything is automated. You don't have to do a thing."

After considerable persuasion, his wife agreed to the plan. She put on his space suit, crawled into the capsule, and waited. All of a sudden, the ship shook, and slowly rose into the air, gathering speed until she floated weightlessly.

Soon, the capsule decelerated so rapidly the woman passed out. She awakened, the capsule floating on the sea, with some man forcefully pressing on her breasts.

"Don't worry, fella," he said. "Just as soon as I can get your balls back into position, you'll be just fine."

221. A Series of Mistakes

Dear Acme Insurance Company,

In answer to your inquiry as to why, in box 13 of your accident reporting form, I stated the cause of my accident as a series of mistakes, I provide the following clarification.

In box 9, I listed my profession as a brick layer. On the day in question, I had just completed laying the last bricks on the roof of a four-story building. It was after five o'clock in the evening, and everyone had left the construction site. I noticed a barrel hoist on the ground floor. I pulled on the rope, and brought the barrel to the top of the building so I could load some extra bricks into it and bring them down to my truck. I tied the rope securely to the stanchion on the ground.

I walked up the four flights of stairs to the roof and loaded the bricks into the barrel, and then walked down the stairs and untied the rope. I bring your attention to box 7, where I listed my weight as 175 pounds. This was my first mistake; the barrel and bricks weighed 300 pounds. My second mistake was to cling to the rope as I was yanked upward.

Somewhere between the second and third floors, I was struck on the head by the descending barrel—which explains the concussion I sustained.

When I reached the roof, I maintained my grasp on the rope and my hands were smashed between the rope and the pulley wheel—which explains the broken fingers and lacerations to my hands. At that time, the barrel struck the ground and its bottom fell out, dropping the load of bricks onto the ground. Still holding tight to the rope, I plummeted toward the ground. Somewhere between the third and second floors, the rapidly rising barrel, now weighing only 50 pounds, struck me—which explains my broken legs.

I made my last mistake when I landed on the pile of bricks on the ground. The pain was so intense, I let go of the rope. The last I remember was the barrel descending and striking me on the shoulders—which explains the broken collar bones.

I hope this letter answers all your questions,

222. A Horse by another Name

A man was seated comfortably in his chair, reading the newspaper, when his wife hit him on the side of his head with a skillet, knocking him to the floor.

When he had recovered his senses, he asked his wife, "Why the hell did you do that?"

She replied, "I found this in your coat pocket."

The man glanced at the note which only had the name *Cindy Moon*. "Good grief, woman, that's the name of the horse I bet on that paid 20-to-1. Remember, I took you out to dinner to celebrate my luck. I kept the name to remember to bet on her if she ran in another race."

"I'm sorry for not trusting you, dearest," she answered. "I apologize for hitting you."

About a week later, the man was again sitting in his chair, reading the paper, when his wife again conked him on the head with the skillet.

When he awoke, he looked at her questioningly, she snarled, "Your horse just called."

223. The Squirrel Invasion

There were five houses of religion in a small Florida town: the Presbyterian Church, the Baptist Church, the Methodist Church, the Catholic Church, and the Jewish Synagogue. Each church and synagogue was overrun with pesky squirrels.

One day, the Presbyterian Church called a meeting to decide what to do with the squirrels. After much prayer and consideration, they determined the squirrels were God's creation and were pre-determined to be there, so they couldn't interfere with God's will.

In the Baptist Church, the squirrels had taken up residence around the baptistery. The deacons met, and decided to scoop up the squirrels, put them into the baptistery, and drown them. The squirrels took a dim view of being drowned, swam out of the tub, and escaped. The next week, twice as many squirrels showed up.

The Methodist Church officers got together and decided they were not in position to harm God's creation. So they decided to humanely trap the squirrels and set them free several miles out of town. Three days later, the squirrels were back.

The Catholic Church came up with the best idea. They baptized the squirrels and registered them as members of the church. Now, they only see them at Christmas, Ash Wednesday, Palm Sunday, and Easter.

Not much was heard about the Synagogue, but they took one squirrel and had a short ceremony called circumcision. They haven't seen a squirrel on the property since.

224. Smart Mexican Maid

The Mexican maid asked the mistress of the house for a raise.

This upset the woman. She inquired of the maid, "Now, Maria, why do you think you deserve a pay increase?"

Maria replied, "Senora, there are three reasons why I want an increase. The first is, I iron better than you."

The wife asks, "Who said you iron better than I?"

Maria answered, "Your husband said so.

"My second reason for asking for a raise is that I am a better cook than you are."

"Did my husband tell you that, too?"

"Yes, Senora.

"My last reason for asking for a raise is that I am a better lover than you."

The woman, now furious, asks, "Did my husband say that as well?"

Maria replies, "No, Senora, the gardener did."

The wife nods her head and says, "I'm glad we had this talk, Maria. How much do you want?"

225. Alabama Boys

Bubba and Billy Joe are walking down a street in Atlanta, when they see a sign reading: Suits $5.00 each, Shirts $2.00 each, Pants $2.50 each.

Bubba says to his pal, "Billy Joe, look here! We could buy a whole gob of these; take 'em back to Stone Mountain, sell 'em to our friends, and make a fortune. Just let me do the talkin' 'cause if they hears your accent, they might just think we're ignorant, and not wanna sell that stuff to us. I'll talk in a slow Georgia drawl so's they don't know we is from Alabama."

They go in, and Bubba says, with his best fake Georgia drawl, "I'll take fifty of them suits at five dollars each, fifty pairs of them there pants at two-fifty a pair, and a hundred of them shirts at two dollars each. I'll back up my pickup . . ."

The owner of the store interrupts, "Ya'll from North Alabama, ain't ya?"

"Well, yeah," says a surprised Bubba. "How'd ya know that?"

"Because, boys, this is a dry-cleaner."

226. Crafty Old Dog

One day an old German shepherd is chasing rabbits in the African veldt, when he discovers he is lost. As he wanders about, he notices a leopard heading rapidly in his direction, with the intention of making the dog his lunch.

The dog thinks *I'm in deep doo-doo now!* Noticing some bones on the ground, the shepherd settles down to chew on the bones, with his back to the approaching cat. Just as the leopard is about to pounce on him, the German shepherd says, loudly, "Boy, that was one delicious leopard! I wonder if there are any more around here?"

Hearing this, the young leopard halts his attack and slinks away into the trees. "Whew," says the leopard, "that was close! That dog nearly got me."

Meanwhile, a chimp who had been watching the whole scene from a nearby tree, figures he can put this knowledge to good use and trade it for protection from the leopard. So he climbs down from the tree and makes a bee-line toward the leopard.

The old German shepherd sees the chimp dashing after the leopard, and figures that something must be up.

The chimpanzee soon catches up with the big cat, spills the beans about the dog's trick, and strikes a deal with animal. The young leopard is furious at being made a fool of, and says, "Hop on my back and see what's going to happen to that conniving canine."

Now, the dog sees the leopard with the chimp on his back. *What am I going to do now?* Instead of running, the dog lies down next to the bones, with his back to the attackers, pretending not to see them. Just as they get close enough to hear him, he says, "Where the hell is that damn monkey? I sent him off an hour ago to bring me another leopard."

Moral: Don't mess with old dogs. Age and skill will always overcome youth and treachery! BS and brilliance only come with age and experience.

227. Overbearing Mother-in-law

Jim's mother-in-law accompanied him and his wife on a safari to Africa. The woman refused to obey any of the directions given by the guide. She would wander away from the campsite in the evening, in spite of the warnings that lions were nearby.

One day, she was particularly obstinate. They'd be told to turn left, and she'd insist they turn right. She'd complain the coffee was too strong, the food unpalatable, or the road too rough. Nothing suited her. When they camped that night, she again wandered off into the night.

Suddenly, Jim heard her scream. With his wife, Jim picked up his rifle and a flashlight, and headed into the brush.

Soon, they came upon his mother-in-law standing in a clearing with a lion circling her. "Don't just stand there," his wife demanded. "Do something."

Jim looked at her and replied, "The lion got himself into this mess. He can damn well get himself out of it."

228. Timing Is Everything

She was standing in the kitchen preparing our usual soft-boiled eggs and toast for breakfast, wearing only the "T" shirt she normally sleeps in.

I walked in, almost awake. She turned to me and whispered, "You've got to make love to me right this moment."

My eyes lit up and I thought *either I'm still dreaming, or this is my lucky day.*

Not wanting to miss the opportunity, I embraced her, and gave it my all, right there on the kitchen table.

Afterward, she said, "Thanks," and returned to the stove, her "T" shirt still around her neck.

Happy, but a bit puzzled, I asked, "What was that all about?"

She explained, "The egg timer is broken."

229. Why Are You Hitting Your Head?

A little three-year-old boy went into the bathroom to go to the toilet.

His mother thinks he's been in there too long, so she goes in to see what's up.

The little boy is sitting on his toilet, reading a book. However, every minute, or so, he puts the book down, grips onto the toilet seat with his left hand, and hits his himself on the top of his head with his right hand.

His mother says, "Billy, are you all right? Why do you keep hitting yourself in the head?"

Billy replies, "I'm fine, mommy. I just haven't done my doo-doo yet."

His mother says, "OK, you can stay here a few more minutes. But, Billy, why are you hitting yourself in the head?"

Billy answers, "It works for ketchup."

230. Lost at Sea

An elderly couple was on a cruise, and the weather was extremely stormy. They were standing on the back of the ship, watching the moon, when a huge wave came up and washed the old woman overboard.

They searched for several days and couldn't find her, so the captain sent the old man back to shore with the promise that he'd notify him as soon as they found something.

Three weeks went by, when the old man received a telegram from the ship. It read: "SIR: SORRY TO INFORM YOU. WE HAVE FOUND YOUR WIFE DEAD AT THE BOTTOM OF THE SEA. WE HAULED HER ON DECK AND DISCOVERED AN OYSTER ATTACHED TO HER. IN IT WAS FOUND A PERFECT BLACK PEARL WORTH $50,000. PLEASE ADVISE REGARDING DISPOSITION."

The old man wired back: "SEND ME THE PEARL. REBAIT TRAP."

231. Looks Can Be Deceiving

A doctor, out on his morning run, noticed an old lady sitting on the front stoop of her home, smoking a cigar. He stopped and walked up to her and said, "I couldn't help but notice how happy you look! What's your secret?"

"I smoke ten cigars a day," she answered. "Before I go to bed, I smoke a nice big joint. Apart from that, I drink a bottle of *Jack Daniels* every week, and eat junk food. On weekends, I pop some meth, have sex, and don't exercise at all."

The doctor enthused, "That is absolutely amazing!" "How old are you?"

"I'm thirty-four."

232. Extra-marital Affair

A man returns home a day early from a business trip. It's after midnight. The man suspects his wife is having an affair and wants a witness when he catches her in the act. For $100, the cabbie agrees to be his witness.

Quietly, they arrive at the home, and the husband and cabbie tip-toe up the stairs, and into the bedroom. The husband switches on the lights and pulls the bed covers back.

There is his wife in bed with another man!

The husband reaches into a drawer in the bedside table, and extracts a gun, which he levels at the naked man's head.

His wife screams, "Don't shoot. I lied when I told you I inherited money. He paid for the Corvette I gave you. He paid for our new cabin cruiser. He paid for your Dodgers' season tickets. He paid for our house on the lake. He paid for our country club membership. He pays the monthly dues."

Shaking his head from side-to-side, the husband lowers the gun. He looks at the cabbie and asks, "What would you do?"

The cabbie replies, "I'd cover his ass with that blanket before he catches cold, and then I'd go sleep on the sofa."

233. Geography of a Woman

Between 18 and 22, a woman is like Africa—half-discovered, half-wild, fertile and naturally beautiful.

Between 23 and 30, a woman is like Europe—well-developed, and open to trade especially for someone of real value.

Between 31 and 35, a woman is like Spain—very hot, relaxed and convinced of her own beauty.

Between 36 and 40, a woman is like Greece—gently aging, but still a warm and desirable place to visit.

Between 41 and 50, a woman is like Great Britain—with a glorious and all conquering past.

Between 51 and 60, a woman is like Israel—has been through war, doesn't make the same mistakes twice, takes care of business.

Between 61 and 70, a woman is like Canada—self-preserving, but open to meeting new people.

After 70, a woman is like Tibet—wildly beautiful, with a mysterious past, and the wisdom of the ages; an adventurous spirit with a thirst for spiritual knowledge.

Geography of a Man

Between 1 and 90, a man is like Iran—ruled by nuts.

234. Symptoms of Old Age

When I went to lunch today, I noticed an old lady sitting on a park bench, sobbing. I stopped and asked her what was wrong.

She said, "I have a 22-year-old husband at home. He makes love to me every morning, then gets up and makes me pancakes, sausage, fruit, and freshly ground coffee."

I inquired, "Well, why are you crying?"

She replied, "He makes me homemade soup for lunch, and my favorite brownies, and then makes love to me for half the afternoon."

"Please, tell me what you're crying about."

She persisted in completing her story, "For dinner he makes me a gourmet meal, with wine and my favorite dessert, and then makes love to me until midnight."

"Lady," I asked sternly, "what do you have to cry about?"

She blubbered, "I can't remember where I live."

235. Misplaced Hearing-aid

Two elderly women were eating breakfast in a restaurant, when one noticed something peculiar about the other. "Mable," Ethyl asked, "do you know you have a suppository in your ear?"

Mable answered, "I have a suppository in my ear?" She pulled it out and stared at it, and then she said, "Ethyl, I'm glad you noticed it. Now I think I know where to find my hearing-aid."

236. Lemon Squeeze

A young woman went to confession. She entered the confessional and said, "Forgive me, Father, for I have sinned."

The priest replied, "Tell me how long has it been since your last confession?"

"A week ago, Father."

"All right," said the priest, "confess your sins and be forgiven."

The young woman said, "Last night my boyfriend made love to me seven times."

The priest thought long and hard. Finally, he spoke, "Squeeze seven lemons into a glass, and then drink the juice."

The young woman looked at the priest questioningly, and asked, "Will this cleanse me of my sins?"

The man replied, "No, but it will wipe that smile off your face."

237. Resisting Temptation

A man entered the confessional, and says, "Father, forgive me, for I have sinned."

The priest asks, "What did you do, my son?"

"I lusted," the fellow replied.

"Tell me more about it," said the priest.

"Father, I am a deliveryman for UPS. Yesterday I was making a delivery in the affluent part of the city. When I rang the bell, the door opened; and there stood the most beautiful woman I have ever seen. She had long blonde hair and eyes like emeralds. She was wearing a sheer dressing gown that revealed her perfect figure. She asked me to come in."

"And what did you do, my son?"

"Father, I did not go in the house, but I lusted. Oh, how I lusted," replied the man.

"Are you married, my son?"

"No, father, I am not

"Your sin has been forgiven," declared the Father. "You'll get your reward in heaven."

"A reward, Father? What do you think my reward might be?" the fellow inquired.

"I think a bale of hay would be appropriate, you stupid jackass."

238. Trying to Do a Good Deed

A man is in bed with his wife when there is a rapping at their front door. He rolls over and looks at the clock; it's half past two in the morning. "I'm not getting out of bed at this time," and rolls over. Then a louder knock follows.

"Aren't you going to answer that?" his wife asks.

He drags himself out of bed; goes downstairs, and opens the door. There stands a man, and it doesn't take the homeowner long to realize the fellow is drunk.

"Hi, there," slurs the stranger. "Can you give me a push?"

"No, get lost. It's half past two! I was in bed," screams the homeowner, and slams the door. He goes back to the bedroom, and tells his wife what happened.

She remarks, "Dave, that wasn't very nice of you. Remember the night we broke down in the pouring rain on the way to pick up the kids from the babysitter, and you had to knock on that man's door to get us started again? What would have happened if he'd told you to get lost?"

"But this guy is drunk!"

"It doesn't matter," explains his wife. "He needs our help, and it would be nice of you to help him."

The husband gets out of bed again, gets dressed, and goes downstairs. He opens the door, but he can't see the man anywhere in the dark, so he shouts, "Hey, do you still want a push?"

He hears a voice call out, "Yes, please."

"Where are you?" shouts the homeowner.

The stranger calls back, "I'm over here, on your swing."

239. Two Kids in the Hospital

Two little boys are in the hospital, lying on gurneys outside the operating room. The first boy leans over and asks, "What are you in here for?"

The second kid says, "I'm here to have my tonsils out, and I'm a little bit nervous."

"Piece-of-cake," the first boy replies. "You've got nothing to worry about. I had that done when I was four. They put you to sleep, and when you wake up, they give you Jell-O and ice cream."

The second kid asks, "What are you here for?"

The first boy answers, "A circumcision."

"Whoa!" the second kid says. "I had that done when I was born; couldn't walk for a year!"

240. Does Your Dog Bite?

A traveling salesman drove up to a farmhouse. There was a hound dog lying on the ground, and an old man, in overalls, sitting on the porch in a rocking chair, reading a newspaper.

The salesman rolled down the car's window and asked, "Excuse me, sir. Does your dog bite?"

The old man looked up over his newspaper and replied, "Nope."

As soon as the salesman stepped out of his car, the dog began snarling and growling. The salesman stepped toward the dog and it attacked the man's arms and legs.

As the young fellow flailed around in the dust, he yelled, "I though you said your dog didn't bite."

The old man muttered, "He ain't my dog."

241. Let's Play a Game

A blonde and a lawyer are seated next to each other on a flight from LA to New York. The lawyer asks if she'd like to play a game.

The blonde, tired, just wants to take a nap, so she politely declines, and rolls toward the window to catch a few winks.

The lawyer persists, and explains the game is easy and will help pass the time. He explains, "I ask you a question, and if you don't know the answer, you pay me $5, and vise versa."

Again, the blonde declines, and tries to get some sleep.

The lawyer, now agitated, says, "OK, if you don't know the answer, you pay me $5. If I don't know the answer I'll pay you $500."

This catches the blonde's attention, and, figuring there'll be no end to this torment unless she plays, agrees to the terms.

The lawyer asks the first question. "What's the distance from earth to the moon?"

The blonde doesn't say a word, reaches into her purse, pulls out $5 and hands it to the lawyer.

"OK," he says, "it's your turn."

She asks the lawyer, "What goes up the hill with three legs and comes down with four legs?"

The lawyer, puzzled, takes out his laptop and searches all his references; no answer. Frustrated, he e-mails all his friends to see if anyone has the answer—no luck there either. He questions the Library of Congress, but comes up with nothing. After an hour, he wakes up the blonde, and hands her $500.

She says, "Thank you," and turns back to get more sleep.

The attorney, more than a little miffed, wakes the blonde and asks, "What's the answer?"

Without a word, the woman reaches into her purse, hands the lawyer $5, and goes back to sleep.

242. Now We Both Got the Makins

A Texan walks into a pharmacy and wanders up and down the aisles.

The salesgirl notices the man, and asks if she can help him.

He answers that he is looking for a box of tampons for his wife.

The salesgirl directs him to the correct aisle.

A few minutes later he appears at the checkout counter and sets down a bag of cotton balls and a ball of string.

The girl is confused, and says, "Sir, I thought you were looking for tampons for your wife."

The Texan answers, "You see, it's like this; yesterday, I asked my wife to pick up a carton of cigarettes for me while she was at the store. She came home with a can of tobacco and some rolling papers. So, hell, I figure if I have to roll my own, so can she."

243. How Did You Make Your Money?

A young reporter, interviewing a rich man, asked him how he made his money.

The rich man fingered his worsted wool vest and said, "Well, young man, it was 1932, the depth of the Great Depression. I was down to my last nickel. I invested that nickel in an apple. I spent the entire day polishing that apple, and sold it for ten cents. The next morning, I invested those ten cents in two apples. I spent the entire day polishing those apples, and by the end of the day I sold them for twenty cents. I continued this system for a month. At the end of the month, I made a profit of $1.37 over our expenses. Then my wife's father died and left us two million dollars."

244. Marriage Counseling

Eileen and her husband Bob went for counseling after 35 years of marriage.

When asked why they were seeking therapy, Eileen went into a passionate, painful tirade, listing every problem they had ever had in the 35 years they had been married.

She went on and on describing the neglect, lack of intimacy, emptiness, loneliness, feeling unloved and unlovable, a litany of her unmet needs during the course of their marriage.

Finally, after allowing this to go on for several minutes, the therapist got up, walked around his desk, and, after asking Eileen to stand, unbuttoned her blouse, embraced her, put his hands on her breasts, and kissed her passionately as Bob watched with raised eyebrows.

Eileen shut up, buttoned her blouse, and quietly sat down as though in a daze.

The therapist turned to Bob and said, "This is what your wife needs at least three times a week. Can you do this?"

Bob thought for a minute and replied, "Well, I can drop her off here on Mondays and Wednesdays, but on Fridays, I play golf."

245. Marketing Strategy

Two beggars are sitting side-by-side, one holding a cross, the other a Star of David.

Many people walk by, look at both beggars, but only put money into the hat of the beggar sitting behind the cross.

A priest comes by, stops, and watches throngs of people giving money to the man with the cross, but nothing to the man with the Star of David.

Finally, the priest goes over to the beggar with the Star of David and says, "My poor fellow, don't you understand? This is a Catholic country; this city is the seat of Catholicism. People aren't going to give you money if you sit there holding a Star of David, especially when you're sitting beside a beggar who has a cross. In fact, they would probably give to him just out of spite."

The beggar holding the Star of David listened to the priest, turned to other beggar with the cross, and says, "Moishe, look who's trying to teach the Goldstein brothers about marketing."

246. Christmas Catalog

Two rednecks were looking at a Christmas catalog and admiring the models.

One says to the other, "Have ya seen them beautiful gals in this catalog?"

The second man replies, "Yeah. They's all beautiful. And look at the price!"

The first one observes, "Wow, they ain't very expensive either. At this price, I'm a buyin' one."

The second man smiles, pats him on the back, and remarks, "Good idee! You order one and if she's as beautiful as she looks in the catalog, "I'll git one too."

Two weeks later, the second redneck asks his friend, "Did ya receive the gal ya ordered?"

His friend replies, "No, but it shouldn't be too long now. I got her clothes yesterday!"

247. Beethoven's Tomb

While walking through an historic graveyard in Vienna, a young man came across the tombstone of Ludwig van Beethoven. He opens the gate in the fence surrounding the gravesite, and sits down on a ledge around the tombstone. As he sits there contemplating the greatness of the man buried here, he hears faint music. Placing his ear against the stone he listens to the strangest musical sounds he has ever heard.

Unable to explain the phenomena, he scurries to a music academy he had noticed earlier, and asks to see the Head Master.

The young man explains the strange sound he has heard emanating from Beethoven's grave, and asks the professor, "Sir, can you explain the source of this sound?"

The professor declares, "I cannot comprehend any explanation. Would you please show me where you heard the strange music?"

The young man leads the Head Master to the gravesite and requests him to press his ear to the stone. Foe several minutes the professor listens to the sound. Suddenly, his eyes widen and he exclaims, "I've got it! The sound is Beethoven's Fifth Symphony played backwards."

"How is this possible?" asks the man.

"It's obvious," relies the professor. "The maestro is decomposing."

248. Strange Pain Killer

The dentist fills a syringe with an anesthetic to give his patient a shot.

"No way! No needles! I hate needles," the patient exclaims.

The dentist starts to connect a face mask and flex tube to the nitrous oxide canister, and the man objects again. "I can't stand a mask covering my face and breathing that gas."

The dentist then asks, "Do you have any objection to taking a pill?"

"No objection," the patient remarks. "I'm fine with pills."

The dentist steps to a cabinet and removes a bottle of pills. "OK, sir, here's a Viagra."

The patient inquires, "I didn't know Viagra worked as a pain killer."

"It doesn't," the dentist answers, "but it's going to give you something to hold onto while I pull your tooth."

249. The Old Indian

A cowboy is riding a fence line along a road when he sees an old Indian lying in the middle of the road, his ear pressed against the dirt.

"What are you doing, old man?" the cowboy asks.

The Native American replies, "One wagon, two horse, one brown, one paint, two women, one white, one Indian."

"Wow!" exclaims the cowboy, "you can tell all that from just listening."

"No," replies the old man. "Women talk, no look, run over me."

(To conclude this volume, I'd like to present the following story.)

250. The Mayonnaise Jar and Two Beers

On the last day of the semester, the kindly philosophy professor stood before his class and said, "Since we will not meet again, I would like to leave you with a couple of truths I hope you will practice for the rest of your lives." He bent down and withdrew a large mason jar and two bottles of beer from under the table.

The students laughed at the sight of the beers. He wordlessly searched under the table and withdrew several other materials which he placed next to the jar and two beers.

With no further conversation he picked up the very large mayonnaise jar, jiggling it as he proceeded to fill it with golf balls. The professor then asked the class if the jar was full. They agreed it was.

He then professor picked up a box of pebbles and poured them into the jar, shacking the jar gently as the pebbles filled in the spaces between the golf balls. Again, he inquired of the class, "Is the jar full now?" They agreed it was.

He then picked up a box of sand, and slowly poured it into the jar. Of course, the sand filled every bit of space. He asked once more if the jar was full. The students responded with an emphatic yes.

"Now," said the professor, as the laughter subsided, "I want you to recognize this jar represents your life. The golf balls are the important things—your family, your children, your health, your friends and your favorite passions. If everything else was lost, and only they remained, your life would still be full.

"The pebbles are the other things that matter, like your job, your house, and your car.

"The sand is everything else—the small stuff. If you put the sand in first, there would be no room for the pebbles or golf balls. The same goes for life; if you spend all your time and energy on the small stuff, you will never have room for the things that are important to you.

"Pay attention to the things that are critical to your happiness. Spend time with your children. Spend time with your parents and grandparents. Take time to get medical checkups. Take your spouse out to dinner. Play another 18. There will always be time to clean the house and fix the disposal. Take care of the golf balls—the things that really matter. The rest is just sand."

One of the students raised her hand and inquired what the beer represented.

"I'm glad you asked," said the professor. He opened the bottles of beer and poured them into the jar. "The beer just shows you that no matter how full your life may seem, there's always room for a couple of beers with a friend."

PLEASE SHARE THESE JOKES WITH YOUR GOOD FRIENDS.

I JUST DID!